GLASGOW CELTIC TWITCHERS' SOCIETY

GLASGOW CELTIC TWITCHERS' SOCIETY

A novella by

Hugh Bradley

ISBN: 978-0-9931143-1-1

Prepared for publication by

DROMBEG BOOKS
Leap, County Cork, Ireland

About the author
Hugh Bradley does a lot of thinking and sometimes he writes stuff down. This book is one in a ground-breaking 'Kango Hammer' trilogy. He is still thinking about Book Two and Three though, and will get back to you on that.

Hugh has always been interested in liberation through random debunking and hasn't yet worked out any beliefs to follow other than Mystic Toast Transformative Hedonism, which he finds to be self-evident and beyond rebuke.

Peregrinatio perpetua?
Naw, mate.

AUTHOR'S NOTE

The characters in this book are real but, for the sake of anonymity, names, personality, events, geographic reality and the story have all been changed.

I include a glossary of some terms that may be unfamiliar to foreign readers:

ah: *I*

ah'l: *I will*

ah'm: *I am*

gallus: *stylishly self-confident*

Buckfast (Bucky): *popular fortified cheap tonic wine made by monks*

The Bhoys: *Celtic Football Club, supporters of Glasgow Celtic*

cheucter: *Gaelic speaker from the highlands and islands*

clebbin: *dirty*

dug: *dog*

fae: *from*

feart: *scared*

fleeto: *gang*

gi'us: *give me.*

haun: *hand*

Jungle: *area of Celtic Park where most vociferous supporters stand*

le'e us alane: *leave me alone please*

mibbe: *maybe*

napper: *head*

Possil(park): *north Glasgow housing scheme*

square slice: *sausage*

swally: *series of long gulps of alcoholic beverage*

tae: *to*

Timaloy: *Celtic fan*

Wegian: *Glaswegian*

whitey: *fainting due to over-indulgence of cannabis/alcohol combination*

widnae: *would not*

wido: *someone not be trusted, off the wall*

wur: *we are*

EPISODE 1

Glasgow Celtic Twitchers' Society

How Tam and Shug's Scoto-African cultural exchange goes a wee bit awry (or away with the birds) and some events leading up to the onset of Ade Adeyobo's drink problem.

For the first time since one million three hundred years bc, Shug found himself sitting high in the canopy of an African rain forest, looking for different varieties of birds with his friend and mental companion of the earth realm, Tam McLaverty. Glasgow was a long way away, and one would have thought there was a real possibility of a panic attack, but strangely, for a while, there had been a comforting cosiness in being up there that he couldn't explain, a monkeyness, an empathy with branches, a retro-genetic understanding.

"There goes another white-tailed chuckle-dancer, Shug!" Tam pointed excitedly below, as happy as if the Bhoys had just scored.

"Yer very good Tam, really ye are, how many is at ye seen?"

"Eleven. They're quite easy to see ye know wi the big tail and the heid that goes from side tae side...are ye keepin a note?"

"Ah am, but who's gonny believe us, wi nae pictures or nuthin? I have it written here tho: *lesser speckled high-tree piper* − 4, *blue-nosed rat-bird* − 5, *bottle-billed sloth-bird* − 2, eh, *greater speckled high-tree piper* − 1. Though ah'm not sure if it was lesser or greater tae be honest."

"Well as long as it's written, that's the main thing, like we're gonny win the treble this year, that's also written." Tam billowed clouds of smoke from his mouth, smiling, as he passed the joint to Shug.

Shug looked at the smooth white paper cone and flicked some ash off the end. The tiniest of neural fear producers in his head started firing, just for a laugh, like. He was beginning to feel out of place. Beyond monkeydom. The insects buzzing round his face were no longer an exotic holiday novelty and the stench of sweat wasn't too pleasant either. Tam's was particularly bad, if the truth be told. He took a long, sweet swig of Irn Bru, thinking about the dwindling supplies left in the carrier bag. He imagined he could hear the shrill whistle of the ice-cream van from a nearby street, but no, it was some class of a bird, calling out from the actual jungle.

"Let's go and have a swally, ah think that's enough twitching fur the day. Ah'v no changed ma money by the way, how much've ye got?" asked Shug.

Tam contorted his red and white bony hand into his damp tight pocket and withdrew a ball of paper.

"Fourteen, mibbe fifteen hundred guinea, but there's no way ah'm sleepin oot again the night. We'll need tae find a place to stay, ah canny face the fuckin horrors man, the beasts, the attempted scavenging, if ah hudnae hit that dug's napper wi a boatle it was fur eatin ma leg."

"It wis a jackal," Shug pointed out. Although deep down he knew it was a dug.

"Fuckin right it wis," Tam snapped back.

"Okay, I agree with ye," Shug went on. "We should have sorted out accommodation before tryin that Tennent's-Mescal-Guaranja-Coca juice snakebite...Ah'm all for this global cultural mish-mash, this eco-diversity, but mibbies we went too far right enough...We are internet giro travellers fae Possil, not Celestine

Prophecy time traveller's fae California."

"Aye...right!" said Tam, enthusiastically confused.

But then again, was there a perfect synchronicity in their adventure? Why was he drawn to visit Tam on that Tuesday afternoon? He had no idea a double giro and rent cheque was expected. Why his search for a cheap flight to Africa on the Community Hall computer?

There was an energy flowing, an anticipation. His flashbacks were of birds he had spotted in Scotland, looking at him, saying something...and now, so many high-tree pipers...lesser and/or greater.

Climbing down through the greenery wasn't so difficult, simply a series of small falls. Each time they were pleasantly surprised not to have plummeted to death by misadventure, but just to have landed on a lower branch. Such unconscious coordination of limbs was remarkable for two men with a long history of kicking kerbs and falling off buses.

They struggled through the thick growth back to the village. Shug wore his Celtic goalie's top and a jumper tied round his waist, and carried the last of their refreshments in a white plastic bag, the cans and bottles banging against his leg as he stretched over and under the branches and creepers.

Shug was an adaptable man; evolution had done well to equip him with the skills to cope with five years of unemployment. He was able to focus on attaining states of energy that were conducive to friendliness and co-operation, while also being able to close down, isolate, and watch a lot of tv in a low-energy state for ten days out of every fourteen.

Numerous liquid chemical attacks on his brain had left him with a psychosis that allowed him to appear to the outsider to be serene and full of human love, whereas internally he was just unaware of the need to compete, achieve, and assert his ego.

Forest became scrub, and looking up they could see waves of heat rising from the sun-scorched ground. The settlement was about half a mile off when Tam took a packet of custard creams from the bag, ate one, and seeing Shug was looking, threw one to him too.

"Race ye tae the toon!" he shouted, and scampered off, bringing up dust and unsettling a nearby group of antelope.

Shug felt uneasy; time slowed as he watched Tam's red mane rise and fall, his arms chugging like a sprinter in slow motion.

An antelope eyed him ."Get him back tae Possil," it seemed to say, before leaping and kicking off into the distance.

Tam stood there, hands on hips.

"C'mon," he coughed. "Enjoy yerself, man, it's a fuckin laugh."

I'm not just here for a laugh, thought Shug, but said, "Your turnin intae a big rasher ye pig ye…c'mon an wull share a few bevies wi the local bad boys."

Roamin in the gloamin
wi a shamrock in ma hand
roamin in the gloamin wi St Patrick's Fenian band!
and when the music stops
fuck King Billy and John Knox,
oh ah'm proud tae be a Roman Catholic.

They unloaded their cargo, and were sitting, singing, beside the small wooden post office shop while a few young boys laughed and played at the front of the shop, throwing stones as part of some game.

A large, suited, bespectacled man, came smiling along the road, walking not unlike a man familiar with gallus attitude.

"Hello, my friend, you sing well, ha! ha! Fuck King Billy, very good, you must be a Tim."

"A Timaloy-bhoy for sure, big man," said Tam and held out his hand.

"Tam McLaverty."

"And Shug Docherty."

"And I am Ade Adeyobo."

"Ye have heard of King Billy then, Ade?"

"Yes, indeed ha ha! I lived in Glasgow, Great Western Road. I was studying at the university for five years, had a total blast so ah did. Glasgow holds an attractive madness for me."

"Ah don't believe it! That's brilliant, eh Shug! Yer man went tae the uni, eh?"

"Aye, very good. Whit knowledge are ye holdin then, Ade?"

"I have a masters in applied animal psychology," said Ade proudly.

A shiver went down Shug's spine as he heard this. Ade held his gaze; there was a sense of combined compassion, a higher vibrational moment,

"The birds," thought Shug. "Something tae dae wi the birds."

"You'll understand this then, Ade," Tam said as he struggled to his feet. "A fuckin antelope looked at me as if ah wis a piece of shit! Whit's that aboot, eh? An antelope! No even a fuckin horse!"

"The animal loves you, Tam, but you seem to have low self-esteem," laughed Ade.

"Well, ye know whit? There's a smack in the jaw comin tae the next animal that loves me, man. Anyways ah disagree, ah think he thought ah wis some kinda lion supporter, wi ma red hair an at."

He turned to Shug. "C'mon, we have tae find an indoors the night. Ade, good tae meet ye, mibbies we'll see ye again. Don't know where, don't know when…"

"Here, gonny gie us a haun up?" Shug asked Ade, who then pulled him up easily.

"I will see you, I am sure. Peace be with you." Ade's voice vibrated mellow and pure.

"Don't ye know it's magic? Ye know, ye'll never beat nine in a row!" sang Tam as he and Shug collided and then began to meander though the village dusk.

Later, the best pals lay in their accommodation, a family-sized, near-empty vegetable store with a good view. Mangoes and yams lay scattered across the dusty floor, and through the open doorway, stars, strong and clean, held their position in the high, huge blackness while calls and vibrations moved through the cooling night air.

Tam was already asleep.

"Would ye get the fuckin butter?" he muttered dreamily, as he turned towards the wall, curled up in his clothes. But he would awaken soon; he never slept well when he wasn't in the top bunk.

"Shug," whispered Tam.

"Shug," louder this time.

"Ah'm fuckin feart man! Shug!"

In his sleep, Shug had been gliding and soaring high above the scorched Savannah; he moved from ear to ear within his head, he was lifted by the hot air, his fingers became boney hooks, his arms wide wings. Getting tired, he flapped weakly. He could see narrow then wide, blinkered then free, he went though his eyes, then out though the eyes of a vulture, thousands of pulses and sharp tingling signals jumping spasmodically from his mind to his spine, an electric charge building, almost enough current to spark a seizure; he tried to scream but was silent except for an *eeeek*. Then he began to fall. Now he was calm, falling to a water-hole; soft, sweet orange water bubbled up, and open-mouthed he dived through, gurgling the quenching cool bru soothing his red raw throat...

"What?!" His ego looked around to see where he had landed this time.

"What is it? What's the matter?"

"Ah'm feart Shug," Tam said, his quivering voice childlike and pleading.

"There might be an early house, wee man." He spoke calmly to Tam.

Shug stretched and scratched, then rolled over until he was looking out the open doorway. The sun had risen just above the rooftops, warm and fresh yellow light illuminating the frequency of matter and so forth.

"Here, would ye have a look, take this." Tam threw some money over. "Get anything," he added.

Shug rolled a crumpled bent cigarette, lit up, and walked out into the village streets. He pretended he knew where he was going. Around him were sounds of morning activity, coughing, children talking, crying, the sound of pots clattering and water pouring. He put his hands through his hair, looked at his watch as if it mattered and sped up.

"God has smiled on me today," he thought, as he turned a corner and saw produce being unloaded from an old battered truck, tins of oil, bags of salt-fish, and bottles of the local wine.

"Burundi Buckfast, praise be to God," he said, and approached the working man.

"Lovely morning again," he said.

The man didn't respond, but raised his eyebrows in some sort of recognition.

"Is yer shop open?" asked Shug.

"Is the question asked?" the man replied.

"Oh aye, eh, see what you mean," replied Shug, but didn't. "How much? The bottles of wine?" The man took two bottles and pressed them to Shug. Close up, he growled,

"Take the wine, drink, then go and talk to your birds! Go and talk to your birds!" he shouted.

Shug tried to make sense of the man's anger as he walked back to rescue his friend from experiencing the true nature of human sentience.

After a few good gulps Tam spoke up.

"Go and talk tae yer birds is it? Mibbies ah'll jist dae that…" Tam was confident again, the wine having been absorbed by the necessary cells. "If he wants trouble, Shug…?" Tam picked up a stick from the ground.

"Naw, Tam…" Shug was dreamy, he seemed to have an aura

of importance. There was something not yet remembered, something true and deep, waiting to be manifest, resting in his mind.

They sat drinking and smoking in the middle branches of a carob tree on the edge of the village, Shug with his back sloping into an accommodating bow, his legs comfortably lying along the top of a thick, smooth, cigar-brown branch.

Tam was wedged between branches in order to balance and to free up his arms as he struggled to role a cigarette, his forehead pressed against a higher branch,

School kids in uniform passed along below, their faces a mixture of fear, fun, and confusion as they saw the two Glaswegians, Shug still in his dayglo goalie's top, and Tam wearing the green and white hoops.

"Ka ka keeeee! Ka ka keeee!" shrieked Tam, moving his arms like chicken wings.

The kids giggled as they continued their way to school.

Shug smiled slowly. His eyes, a clear light blue, open and innocent, gazed gently out towards the deep, high green carpet of forest. They were at the edge of the forest. There had to be an edge somewhere and this was it; it was therefore a place of ecological importance.

Scientists often came to Baliglower to collate and measure, and generally turn things into numbers. Because of this a quality road had been built, from the airport 100 miles north in Ambollo Gola. It was still unusual, however, for travellers to get here. Shug and Tam would not have made it had they planned it; instead, in inebriation, they fell into a chain of causes and conditions that carried them all the way from Possil, the final leg of the journey in the back of a farmer's truck, returning from the market. Tam was disappointed when they arrived, as he was expecting a beach; he was more than adept at ornithology, having developed an obsession one acid-fuelled summer, but he had little grasp of geographical reality.

Shug swept his blond curls from his face,

"Do you remember our first day we stood in the Jungle, Tam?"

"Brilliant, aye," he enthused "The best 'walk-on' ah'v ever seen an heard, Bucky in the back pocket, beat Ab'rdeen 3-0, an got aff wi Sheila Coyne that night…and even hud change for a bag of pakora on the way hame."

"Do you remember how green the green wis? The scarves? The grass?"

"Green's green, Shug! Different shades, grant ye."

"Naw, Tam, there was a higher vibration, love made the green greener, an ah'm getting that same vibe here, now…Tam?"

"Aye?"

"Is there a wee bit left?"

Tam placed his wine in a hollow, and pulled out his sweaty jeans pocket lining. A wee brown ball of hash popped out and fell, Tam almost following it. Underneath them flew a native Burundian macaw, as if in slow motion as it gulped down the hash bit.

"Ex-cell-ent," it squawked, as it flew off.

Shug and Tam stared open mouthed at each other. "What-the-fuck-is-that? That bird sounds like it's fae Greenock!" exclaimed Tam.

Shug blinked, something stirred in his mind. He became open to the recognition that action must follow intuitive energy – there was something he must do in this situation. An invigorating, holistic shiver seemed to cleanse his toxic body.

"Tam," he announced, "Ah'm gone tae talk tae the birds."

"Aye, you tell the barst'rdn birds," Tam began, but fell forward, and hugged the tree. "Ah'm havin a whitey, come back an get us."

[10]

Shug dropped from the branch, his legs bent, then straight. He brushed some flakes of bark from him, then retied his laces, making the bows of equal size, and strode off with grace and purpose towards the rainforest.

Creepers glistened gold and green, heavy moisture laden leaves caressed him as he passed, leaving a cooling breeze floating round his neck. Torch beams of sunlight illuminated his path and clumps of solid earthy roots seemed to rise like stepping stones under his feet. The forest thinned slightly and the individual giants that held the breathing, decaying, growing, eco-system together could be more clearly seen. Thousands of busy insects wove patterns, turned and span around the air, but none came within a ten-foot arc forward of his head. Shug flowed through the forest; his face glowing with the beauty of relaxed intent, he was present and aware, true to this moment and all moments, all moments being one.

He lay on a cool stone slab, gravity strong and comforting. His feet and legs relaxed, his back heavy, his hands seemed to open as if from a fist as his head gave up its tension; his mind had a clarity, in tune for the first time with the simple rhythms of the universe.

The sound of wing flaps and calls began, short flights and landings. Shug's eyes were closed, and the purity of sound went through him. Then, after some unhealthy sounding coughing, the speaking arose:

"Le'e us alane…le'e us alane…squawk!" the birds chorused, more and more joining in. "Le'e us alane…le'e us alane… squawk!…le'e us alane…le'e us alane"

And then quiet, until, "Fuckin right – we are ra peeeppullll… squawk."

"Gi'e us a chip…squawk!…gi'e us a chip…"

"Gi'e us a chip…squawk!…gi'e us a chip…"

"Ah'v nae chips!" shouted Shug at last, as the high pitched incessant shrieks pierced his head.

"Ye ate the lot, ya bastard!" replied a bird. Others joined in, "Ate the lot…ate the lot…ate the lot…"

This is mad, Shug thought,and then out loud, "Am ah some kind of nutter?"

"Total nutter…total nutter," retorted a large, smug macaw.

The birds began to swoop down to Shug, almost touching his face as they passed, their big yellow eyes meeting his fear-struck gaze. One by one they implored him,"Put the stick doon…put the stick doon…"

"Hand it over…squawk!…hand it over…" and "The big man's no happy…no happy…no happy."

"What do ah need to do? Whit's the message?" Shug asked, nervous as a giraffe on a conveyor belt.

"Change or die, wee man, change or die…squawk!" And, "Who's a stupid lookin animal then? Squawk! Manky parrot! Manky Parrot!"

At last they dispersed, wing beats fading away into the dense growth, leaving behind the hum of insects, risen to an angry buzzing. Hellish fear- filled screeching vomited from nearby monkeys, pulling at their own hair and jumping against trees.

Shug was sweating, and dizzy."Oh God, in the name of Christ," he shouted. His muscles ached and spasmed. Sitting up, his heart raced fast and weak; he felt outside his head and needed to be inside, but not trapped, not open, not here. Blinking and clicking his tongue, he held his head, then put his shaking hands out to touch his legs. A huge shining purple beetle fell onto his lap. Jumping up, he shook it off, screamed, and began running, his face slapping against sharp, stinging plants. He fell, then got up again, lost.

"Which fuckin way?" A heavy fly battered into his eyeball.

There was something up his nose. He scrambled along on his hands through heavy, foul-smelling, worm-full mud. He began to cry, sobbing, just a wee boy lost, and scared, and wanting his mum, his Dad. Even, God, a small whiskey.

At last,Shug felt a comforting, loving hand on his head.

"You're all right, Shug, my friend, you're all right." It was Ade again, the Glasgow animal psychiatrist. He helped Shug to his feet and hugged him, they were slowly synchronising their energies, Shug finally stopped shaking, somehow accepting the situation and Ade felt a bit weird, and thirsty, with an unknown longing creeping through him, but was sure he was able to handle it.

"Come," Ade said and led him out to the edge of the forest and into his jeep.

Ade drove back along a bumpy track to his house in the village. Shug accepted a cool drink, took in his new surroundings and felt safe again. He lit a roll-up and returned to the world he knew, familiar feelings, but somehow with a new clarity, a change.

Ade took a beer from the fridge and guzzled it down.

After a brief silence, Ade felt he better tell his story.

"I didn't expect such an effect, such…emotional charge,"Ade began. Shug raised his eyebrows.

"This is something to do with you," Shug said. "Ah kinda knew it would be."

"Yes, there is more going on, Mr Docherty, than my science can explain, but let me give you some context."

"Context wid be good, right enough."

Ade opened another bottle of Tenants Super-Duper (for export only) Lager.

"This is good stuff…eh…need to get some more for later… oh yes, I was saying, some context…I have been studying the effect of a released, formally captive bird, upon a group of Burundi macaws, The particular bird I released, I brought back myself from Scotland after I finished my degree.

"Where in Scotland?" Shug asked.

"Paisley," Ade replied, bringing an understanding nod from Shug.

"The owner developed a drug psychosis and could no longer bear the bird's chatter. I met them both on the train to Glasgow. I was returning from observing a sheep dog trial near Dalry, which had ended in a sectarian bloodbath, but that's another story." Ade shook his head seriously at this memory.

"Anyway, on the train he saw me from the far end of the carriage and broke into a big mad smile. He bounced along the corridor and came right up to me. 'Its yours! Of course!' he said, and pressed the cage to me, and then, as an afterthought. 'Just £20, big man, treat it well, mind.' I gave him the money. He was delighted and grasping the note returned to his seat, but turned and added, 'Ah recommend a rehab by the way.'

"Well, strange as it may seem, it suited my purposes. I saw immediately it was a native Burundian macaw, and I knew there was scope for a study programme using this bird.

"Ah can see that, aye." Shug went along with the story.

"When I got to Baliglower, only a year a go now, I released the bird with a tracking mechanism and recorded events. The mimicry began after a pecking order was established. The released bird was particularly aggressive and soon had a number of birds as underlings. Then all the birds began coming into the village. 'Any jellies, ya bastard?' they shouted at the locals and 'Switch that shite aff!' when people watched the community TV. My people were most upset. When I translated for them they wondered why a bird of the forest would need a relaxing pill. Our great elder of the village advised that we get some Scottish people to talk to them. His

[14]

dream vision was of Billy Connolly telling jokes up a tree, wearing our traditional war battle clothes of green white and orange. Well, we didn't get Connolly but he reached yourselves."

Shug was quiet. Ever since those days of watching Daktari, Saturday mornings in his pyjamas, he felt he had a role to play in Africa; he could never have guessed how it would happen, but that was the start of his intuitionus profundus, which was to guide him on through his teenage years.

"I am sorry it upset you so…I wanted to ask for your help, possibly to speak peacefully to this bird."

Shug knew this was about more than just mimicry. These birds had become agitated. The energy from this new bird, it was a decadence radiation, an individualism that was weakening Burundi macaw consciousness. This unspoken, inherent, true sense of being had become corrupted by the seeing of itself, self-consciousness through seeing difference. Shug had memories of the Jungle, times when he *was* the Celtic support, he *was* 60,000 people, he *was* history and 'The walk on – it *was* a natural spontaneous outpressing of God as earth energy, yet it didn't last beyond a few minutes until individuals appeared again, egos and fear and choice.

Shug was reminded of his awakening…

"If I could help you, Shug?" Ade asked.

"Yes, Tam needs to get home. Could we stay here tonight, and maybe you could take us to the airport in the morning? I could make a tape for you to play to the birds, a peaceful voice…"

"Yes, of course," Ade smiled. They clasped hands.

"Nice tae be nice," Shug said.

"I love you, man, you're like a brother, visit anytime, okay? We will enjoy a few drinks maybe, a game of cards, sing a song or two?"

***

[15]

Possil Community Hall, Glasgow.

Tam pulled himself up out of the hedge and continued towards the off-sales. He clocked Shug outside the Hall.

"Bottle-billed sloth-bird − 2, ya big plook ye!" he shouted across the street.

"Tree pipers − nil," Shug replied.

Tam meandered over, hugged Shug, and moving round to the front of the table where Shug was standing, he peered, curiously perplexed, at the posters taped to it.

"Green...Peace? Whit's this Shug? The Provos? Ye watch yerself, Shug, ye take things too seriously so ye do...c'mon wi me for a swally."

"Thanks Tam, ah'm no so thirsty these days. Here, take this."

"No thirsty?" Tam wondered about his pal's strangeness.

Shug put a *Recycle Reclaim Re-use* sticker on Tam's chest.

"Very good, Shug." Tam tried to twist his jumper to read it, then shrugged and shuffled off, turning with a clenched-fist salute.

"Roamin in the Gloamin..."

Shug held up his open-palmed hand, and shouted after him, "Aye, keep a hold a that shamrock, wee man! You wouldn'y be ready to let go..."

EPISODE 2

Cooking for TV

How Tam and Shug look to night classes as a solution to their existential angst. Alas, in a slip of concentration, Shug loses consciousness. His pal revives him with a combination of sentient matter therapy, and pure annoyance. On Shug's awakening, both men vow to lead a simpler life and set off for Skye, until Shug is harassed for non-payment of overdue library fines. Shug refuses to pay, and instead inspires a revolutionary optimism within the ranks of the Highland and Islands Work Placement Division, and some nervous loyalty from Tam. Thus, in a show of pan-Celtic Communist unity, they embark on a propaganda quest to London.

"Fancy a roll an square slice, Shug?"

"Aye, why not Tam? Go easy on the free radicals tho, eh? Ah'm turning into a roll an sausage slowly but surely here." He slapped his quivering belly as Tam brought out a frying pan from under the grill.

"Whitever you say, Shug." Tam wielded a bent fork as he conducted his words. "Ah widnae pit doon naebody that wis tryin tae better things for the working man. Now, let's prepare here, I tend tae use a fresh roll fae Auld's the Bakers. This wan ah bought masell yesterday and have had it resting on tap of the fridge there, beside ma maw's odereaters, jist till ah'm ready for it."

Tam was getting very chatty these days and it was becoming a delight to sit in his kitchenette and observe him in action. Since taking up meditation, Shug was developing a real interest in absolutely everything that went on around him. Last week, he had spent three days in Glasgow Central Station, watching the comings and goings and counting how many different facial expressions there were (twenty-seven in total) and only left when his mate's seventy-two hour shift as a security guard ended, to be replaced by somebody that gave a fuck, who consequently moved Shug out of the station. "Stoap starin at the passengers, ya dobber," he exclaimed officiously.

Tam continued in his talkative manner, Shug looking up from the chair in grateful wonder at this culinary spectacle.

"There's no need tae melt the lard first, and its perfectly okay tae place your Lorne sausage on top of the delicious, cold, white congealment.

"If you have an electric cooker wi jist wan ring left that isnae scunnered, then obviously use that wan, but if ye have a choice a wid always go for the ring at the front right, as it's the easiest tae figure oot how tae turn on. Turn it right up and leave it a while, till ye hear it splatterin and, in the meantime, ye can be getting on wi butterin the rolls."

Tam held the crusty flour-dusty rolls, one in each hand, a look of surreal seriousness on his face, and turned to Shug,

"McKechnie's rolls would be just as good if ye canny get tae Auld's, but do remember that wee Sheila Flood works there, and she wouldnae win Hygienic Food Operative of the Year Award... as you well know, Shug."

"Aye, that's enough, we agreed no tae mention Sheila."

"Can't remember agreeing, ma friend."

Tam opened the fridge, confidently and smoothly, and brought out one of the cans of Super T, but thought better of it and put it back and continued.

"If you're completely into this big time, ye might remember tae take the butter oot ae the fridge about an hour earlier to soften it, but ah'm sure that's a wee bit advanced for us here today. Just put a lump of butter in the middle of each roll, preferably without bits of foil attached. Yer maw's strawberry jam might still be clingin tae the butter, but if anything, this will enhance the experience…"

Tam wiped his hands on his jeans legs enthusiastically, and tucked in his (too big) *Visit Glasgow Zoo* t-shirt. The lion's face was so similar to Tam's that Shug often got great reincarnationist hope from seeing it.

Shug was drooling, having been fully turned on by the wordy enhancement of reality that Tam had been indulging in. There was a new quality to Tam's speech and manner these days. Normally Shug would have recognised it as purely unself-conscious munchies behaviour. There was no way though that Tam would get stoned without at least a token sharing with Shug and anyway, Tam knew that he was not allowed to be tempting Shug away from his new, clean living, drug-free reality trip. No, it was something else entirely and he couldn't quite put his finger on it, till he looked down at the kitchen table and became aware of a leaflet there.

POSSILPARK ADULT EDUCATION PROGRAMME
CLASSES STARTING SEPT 2001
Thai kick boxing for relaxation.
Conversational English for Quiet Folk.
Gaelic Poetry (please note students must have first attended 'What Cheucters speak' held last yr.)
Cooking for TV.

Cookin for tv? Of course! So fuckin obvious, Tam out every Tuesday night between seven and nine, and now all this talking at him likes he's an audience. Shug smiled inwardly...fuck and he's actually, for once in his life, quite good at it. Apart from the bird watching, in which he was undisputed fucking best at in Glasgow by a long chalk (fourteen muppet dancers and a ring-necked polo warbler on the same day). In general though, Tam was resigned to being not very accomplished at useful human skills, indeed he was known to be a sorry example of complex multi-faceted humanity.

But now he'd turned his hand to this cookery talk show adventure, a complicated interweaving of munchie talk, terrible interpersonal skills, and a penchant for exaggerating the importance of snacks, producing just the right nonsense for this caper.

Not letting on he had become aware of the reasons for Tam's behaviour, Shug piped up,

"Are they no ready yet? Smell cooked tae me, Tam."

Tam raised a suspicious eyebrow as he turned from the frying pan.

"Can ye see the fat globules in the sausage meltin and mixin wi the lard in the pan? Can ye see the edges of the square slice curl and shrink? Naw ye canny, so fuckin shut it, Shug, ye don't know whit yer talking aboot, okay?"

"Eh, okay, sorry Tam, ah'm just sayin nae need tae get offended. As a matter of fact ah'v been enjoying listening to ye talk aboot it, you seem to jist lose yourself in the process, you seem really tuned in" –Tam's wild red eyebrows began to relax – "and ah know you do a great roll an sausage, ye always have, Tam, the hale street knows it."

"Really?"

"Aye!"

"Ah mean really, really? Do ye like listening tae me goin on and on here?" Now he began to look like the lion from the yellow brick road. "Cos ah'm a scared man, Shug, and ah'm just trying

[20]

to…to keep some kind of decent rhythm going in ma head, or else a get aw feart again."

Tam trembled and wheeked the sausage square slices out of the pan and into the rolls and sat down with Shug at the table. As an afterthought, he put Shug's roll on a saucer and kind of positioned it nicely in the middle. With a wee nod to say, "Well, get tore in ma friend", Tam took a bite and looked thoughtful as he minced it up in his mouth, looking quite the connoisseur, till his top plate slid out and he got some soggy roll stuck above his palate. Sucking it away and smacking his lips he beamed a greasy grin across the table that was meant to say, "We are sharing this journey, and have experienced much together, and I appreciate your presence in my life" but came across to Shug as, "I am a fuckin gonner. Too mental tae carry on, crossed the statutory line, and as my mate, it's up to you proceed with putting another Psychiatric Section in process."

Shug, although understanding of his pal's pain, was not prepared to do that again, however. All the evidence from these past years seemed to suggest that Tam just needed to feel safe, and this was difficult in the absence of a continuous supply of alcohol, cannabis and temazepam. A spell in the hospital usually allowed Tam even greater degrees of non-responsibility; he liked nothing better than the tea trolley, the medicine round, and the interest of others in his inability to think the way they thought he ought to. But they could not take away his sense of being an outsider, they could never do that.

Shug reached over and placed his hand on Tam's shoulder, giving it a small squeeze.

"Tasty, Tam, very tasty…well done pal." He then held up the leaflet.

"Listen Tam, whits this aboot, night classes an that? You doin anything? Any recommendations?"

"Hey! Hawd oan Shug a meant to say to ye, hawd oan mate, listen, ah do that cookery, see it there? Well, there's an old sayin, better a single man in a cookery night class than a month of night clubs – see whit ah'm getting at?" The grin again.

"Yeah, Tam, well good thinking mate, and you've fair took tae it ah must say. Anything a wid be interested in? Mibbie no the cookin, don't want to cramp yer style there. Meditation Advanced sounds interesting, eh?"

"But you dae meditation already Shug, don't ye? Ah mean, your so fuckin meditative sometimes ah wonner if yer hidin drugs fae yer best pal, ye know?"

A green and yellow double-decker bus stopped at the bus stop outside the window. Shug's gaze was matched by a jealous, disturbed looking old guy sat on the top deck, seeming to long for company and a roll and square slice.

Shug could not take the man's pain and looked away; it touched something in him that he didn't want to feel. He turned his attention back to Tam.

"Ah know ah do it already, Tam, ah can get well mellow, fae breathin in air and countin and listenin, an all the techniques ah had to learn over the years when a couldny get aff ma arse an go and get some money for drugs. But what age am ah noo, eh? Twenty six, twenty six years and whit can a say to ma maw that would make her pleased wi puttin in aw that effort, eh? Aw those sacrifices she made. Not much Tam. And ah want to please her…

"Ye know what she did the day ma da was carted off? Ah know ye aw slagged me aboot her at school, Mystic Meg, and Woo the Witch of Stoneybrae Road, ah did maself. Anyway, she put a few Tarot cards on the table, and slipped two out, ah don't know much about this, but wan she said wis a major arcana card. *Art* she said, the other she said was the *knight of cups*. Anyway, she told me I would see Dad again. Something about an angel, and both us standing on a rock bottom.

"All I could say was, 'Whit aboot the pocket money, ma? An whos gonny get the fish an chips on a Friday?' She made sure ah didnae go without, Tam, wi a few pickled onions flung in as well. Ah know she loves me Tam, but whit a great surprise for her, eh, if a wis tae be really good at something? Like excellent at meditation even? High Swami Buddha Lama The Shug. Ye know?"

Tam listened in silence, wanting to understand. He pushed an enrolment form over to Shug and took out a Celtic pen from a Celtic pencil case that lay on the Celtic tablecloth.

"Here, sign yer name, Shug, do the meditation, we can go there the gither tomorrow night, ma maw and your maw will be the happiest maws in Possil, no just cos we've stayed oot a jail for these past years, but because, well because we were brave enough tae be different, brave enough to take a wee look at the inner workins of the mind…aw…ah feel a bit fuckin funny again, ma heed, mind whit the fucks that, aw…naw ah feel sick…"

Crawling on his hands and knees, Tam made his way through the living room to his bedroom, pausing at the bar fire to light a cigarette; he remained mesmerized for a while by the fake light that danced slowly and regularly behind the plastic coal. A large red glow, moving up behind the black plastic rocks, small glow behind, large glow again, not so large, smallest yet…large red glow, moving up, small glow behind, large glow again, not so large, smallest yet…for a moment Tam was his true self, ego-less and at one, at peace with the bar fire and with all that is, beyond time: essence itself.

A familiar voice began to resonate at the edges of his consciousness.

"Get tae bed, Tam, have a wee lie doon there, mate. Ah will see ye tomorrow, nae thinking now, have a look at yer Seabirds of Europe book ah got ye, The fuckin puffins, mate, have a look at yon puffins."

Helping Tam into his bed, Shug said his goodbyes and let himself out. Mrs McLaverty would be home soon enough, and it was never easy talking to her when he was straight and sober; he would feel about seven years old and guilty about not being at school.

Shug let himself out into the barren, car-less roads, and felt the cool dampness of the air around him. "All these buildings full of people, electric bar fires, drugs and rolls an sausage," he thought. "Perched on a hill top in Glasgow, what the fuck for…"

He strolled into town, he could see all the east and south of Glasgow stretch out below him, Parkhead in the distance, a big Celtic spaceship, and to his right behind the Western Road, the university, all cleverly twirly and old. Behind that he could make out the shining silver gleam of the science museum, a beacon of the Scottish study of moving parts and the meaning of things. Under his feet the pavement, tough and hard, laid by some strangers' hands, some years ago, a socialists gift for the walking people of Glasgow.

As he moved down hill he was entering Off-Sales and Refined Carbohydrates Land. Macaroon bar wrappers blew in the chill wet wind; one flapped up and landed flat against Shug's mouth, allowing him the sweet taste of sticky white coconut sugariness, just for a second, before it blew off on its kissing travels. Here and there, older guys, like extras left behind from some film set that departed years ago, moved meaninglessly but proudly between bookie's shop and pub. Some lingered outside, grey and purple/red, their native species.

Lost in his new optimism and looking forward to the class,

Shug temporarily lost his awareness: seeing a guy in a vivid Celtic away-top across the road, and thinking it was the wee green man, he ventured into the path of oncoming traffic to be hit by a rugby player's Land Rover. Flung, like the fragile lump of humanity he was, and crunched, folding and contorted, split-bloodied and unconscious, he lay, head against the kerbstone, internally functioning but unawake.

At the same moment Tam fell off the bed and landed on his young brother's Scalextric set, his foot accidentally pressing the trigger and allowing a car to drive up and jab him sorely on the nose. Such an awakening, although not unusual, seemed to get Tam thinking, and he could sense his pal being in danger. He had these intuitive visions rarely, the last time being when Buckfast Boy won the 4.30 at Kempton park.

Tam spoke quickly to his mum as he raced out the door: "Need tae help ma pal, ah need tae help ma pal. Shug's hurt, ah know it."

"You two no hud enough trouble?" Mrs McLaverty exclaimed while drying her hands on her Highland Cow t-towel; she loved Scotland, just felt that the people ruined it. "About bloody time the pair of ye jumped the train to London, youz have me heart roasted, so ye do."

Tam arrived at the accident scene and was informed by the local shopkeeper that Shug had gone to the Royal Infirmary.

The Holy Mary Hospital for Sick Tims would have been better, but Shug must have been in no position to argue.

Tam made his way to the Royal, taking care to avoid the psychiatric wing. The temptation to relinquish responsibility and self-momentum was great at these times, times of harsh reality, times of external factors impacting on his mind, ah! *Mind* again, fuck sake was there no getting away from it?

Shug was in Ward 14, bed 27. Tam approached slowly to the

desk, unsure as to how to look like a visitor and not a patient. A nurse explained to Tam that Shug was stable but hadn't regained consciousness. Tam had seen his pal many times in that condition, but this time there was a clinical voidness to Shug's face. "Like a Paisley Buddie. Soulless, bereft of higher spiritual imagination," he said out loud, surprising himself with his parochial prejudice and socioreligious insights.

Mrs Docherty was there, sitting close to Shug, crying while she told him about how she was in Mrs Stewart's when the police arrived to tell her what happened, and how Mrs Stewart adjusted the photo frame of John and Andy graduating from college on the window sill as she saw Mrs Docherty to the door. "Ye poor thing," she said, the hint of an evil smile creeping across her face as she closed the door.

Tam approached the bed, jelly-legged and sweating.

"Ah will come back in a while, Mrs Docherty" He looked down and made to leave, but she got up and offered Tam the seat.

"You stay here, Tam, and I'll be back in a while." She smiled and patted him on the shoulder. "You're a good boy, Tam McLaverty, sit a here a wee while, talk yer nonsense to my son, mibbies that's what he's needin to hear."

"Aye, Mrs McLaverty, ah'll do ma best, will tell him what ah'm thinking like, he might wake and correct me, eh?" Tam winked at her anxious face.

"Whitever son, I'll be back in a wee while."

Tam looked edgy and coy, finding it hard to talk at first with the proximity of the patient – "Ah mean, whit can ye say?" He glanced at his friend's blank face. "Well fuck it, ah'll be maself just let it flow, ma friend, aye, just let it flow.

"Eh, Shug, yer no looking too good mate, eh…huvnae woke up ah suppose, bit of ye no working like, well not to worry. Ah suppose ye might be in a deep meditative state like, eh? Ye might no even need that Meditation Advanced, eh? Saved a few bob there mate. Wise ye'll be when ye wake up, ah'm sure. Eh, ah'll just have a wee Alka Seltza while ah'm here, Shug, have a couple in ma pocket here. Ah'd gee ye wan, but your no in the mood, naw, ah can see that, mibbie later, eh? There we go…whit a wee fiz…excellent, how that's no bigger than Coke or Irn Bru ah don't know."

Tam gulped it down with one eye on the neighbouring patient before continuing. "Did I tell ye whit happened Saturday, Shug? Ah was oot the backyard, studying the sparrows, actin aw dead weird so they are, like doin a wee dance in front of me, like tryin to tell me something, ye know the kind of thing?

"Well, there's me, tryin tae work it oot, a wee shuggle to the left, a wee step back, turn in a circle, shuggle to the right, and ah huvnae a clue, till ah look more in its eyes, and then ah just got it, man! Got whit he wis doin…know whit he wis tryin tae say tae me? 'Nae mare kebabs', fuck, ah understood where he was comin fae and it was, it was…a holy moment, Shug. 'Nae mare kebabs', eh?

"See, wee Peter upstairs hus been thowin the remains of his kebabs oot the winday, an fur a while the fuckin sparrows were lovin it, but they canny take any mare man, they're aw fat and greasy roon the lips, well it's no lips, more of a beak of course? Anyway, ah says tae Peter that night when ah bumped into him on his way hame, 'Oy,' ah says. 'Whits your problem?' he says. 'You kill any o they wee sparrows wi yer lamb donner an ah'll fuckin brain ye, right?'

"He's some wido though, looks at me like he husnae a scoobie, so a just tap ma head wi ma finger. 'Ah'm no daft,' ah says."

Looking beside him, Tam could see that the next-door patient, a young fellow-housing-schemie, ravaged by the heroin by the looks of things and happily attached to a morphine drip, is throwing faces across the ward and gesticulating, *rippin the pish oot a Tam big time,* as they say. Tam goes hush for a second, uneasy.

"Well Shug, ah best be off, your mibbie tired there pal, and yer maw will be back soon, ah think she's just off in the smokin room."

He takes Shug's hand in his, nearly in tears as he looks at his friend. "Yer nails are clebbin, big man," he says, and flings it back down.

It had become too much for Tam and he was close to a severe psychotic episode; he could never handle stress, it easily tipped him over into fear and unreality. But he had hatched a small plan to give himself some peaceful respite, anything to avoid the pain.

Shug was separated from his clebbinness though. He was currently looking down on himself, and down the nurses' tops as he floated in non-physicality. Trying to imagine the once knowable feeling of matter and momentum, but unable, he drifted on the ephemeral breeze, unshocked by the simple truth of spiritual intelligence; he was resonating in a symphony of understandable music. Spaces there were none.

Just the tiniest of sparks would bring him back, the thinnest thread of sentience, processed, sub-atomic transference, back, back, memory of the cat digging its claws in the bed, understanding its form, back, mmmm, nnnn, back, wake up, a stone so dense, a gurgle of water, cold steel, holding, back, smell, prawn cocktail crisps bag just opened, back, the shudder of being, twilight, late shift, police, Tam, Tam pretending to be a patient, back there, turning up the morphine device, clatter, visitors, a woman shouting "He's not my Jim! Where's my Jim? Who the fuck is this?" Back.

Tam, swallowing the morphine solution, getting warm, safe, free from responsibility, drifting up, above and beyond the clattering, where Shug is. Where's Shug? Is that you, Shug? The wee birds, Shug, aww flying man, smooth quiet gliding flying man...

Blood splattering as the drip is removed, doctor withdrawing the tube, the warm saltiness splashes on Shug's mouth, taste, alive taste, taste alive, zooming through the whiteness of the interface, and...sore, fuckin sore, aw doctor and police, man whit the fuck, ma head aww sore and confused, Tam and Police and Doctor and Alive.

Tam was handcuffed and led out of the ward, but just as he was leaving, Shug started singing, very, very quietly, but amplified by the moment that it was:

Westering ho! With a song in the air,
na na na na and it's good bye to care,
Westering ho and ah huvnae a care, over the sea to Skye...

A wink from Shug to Tam, a trusting glance, connection.

Remote cottage at the foot of the Cullin Mountains, Isle of Skye

Shug looked up from his book, Descartes – *The Meditations*.

"Hows yon Puy lentils comin on Tam? Ah'm starving here mate." Shug forgot he would be in line for a complicated answer.

"Well, Shug. Yon Puy lentils are buzzin man, absolutely fuckin quantum leapin aboot the pan, ah swear there's mare in there noo than there was when a started, how does that work? Fuck knows. But it's gallus as fuck but. There's a tumbling an revolvin, fly wee jinks an volcanic eruptions, spacey bubbles and warm smellin softness, earthy combustion, sauce fae self-smoothiness, opening spreadin and joinin, lentils are mental, Shug, remember that, ah mean it."

"And, eh, ready?"

"I'll sense when the time has come, ye canny rush lentils ma friend."

After Shug recovered from his accident and Tam recovered from his psychotic episode, they decided to leave Glasgow and all its chaos behind them, and check out the Housing Benefit situation on the Isle of Skye. It wasn't too difficult. In Portree SPAR they saw an advert, *Cottage for rent, superb views, near a stream of fresh running water, unemployed Wegians welcome*

Shug closed his book slowly and placed it on the window sill. Looking out, he could see a golden eagle glide and fly, high amongst the craggy steepness of the Red Cullins. It was a snapshot scene that challenged him, a context that he wanted to be comfortable in, but still it seemed somehow bereft of his sweety shops and pubs, broken-up playgrounds and football tops, hospitals and buses and grannies and carrier bags and Bucky, pies and the Daily Record.

"This land is my land, this land is your land." He smiled, as the synchronous strains of Woody Guthrie became louder.

"But ah don't huv the shoes fur it," thought Shug, the music from the cottage radio fading away once again.

Beep! Beep!

The two pals were startled by the loudness just outside the window. Tam jumped over to the door and looked out.

A large man stood at the door, a scraggly plaid around him, pinned together with a badge that said 'Alistair McCloud, Highlands and Islands Mobile Library'.

"Are you Shug Docherty? "

"Naw," said Tam, "Whit ye want him fur?"

"Descartes' *Meditations on First Philosophy — in which the Existence of God and the Distinction Between Mind and Body are Demonstrated*. It's overdue two months, is he there?"

"Aye, hang on".

"Shug! Yer man wants his book back."

Shug looked up.

"Ask him how the fuck he knows ah'v got the book, when ah might huv gien it back yesterday while he was dreamin."

Tam relayed the question.

"Shug, he says he has memory of the difference between dreamin and no dreamin and the fuckin library card husnae been stamped, so gie him the fuckin book back."

Shug looked thoughtful.

"Ask him, when he was whirlin aboot at last night's ceilidh, did he dance or was he the dance?"

Tam asked.

Shug could hear the silence then a melodic voice, then something else entirely.

Tam came back in.

"He says he did in fact feel like the dance, the music and his body were unified, and that in those moments he had no doubts but felt free and most alive. He then started wailin like a wild man, an noo he's pickin up rocks and hurlin them doon the brae, an he's shoutin, 'Saor Alba anis!' and 'I am not a trainee library clerk!' and, eh, 'We should not be eatin fish fingers and macaroni pies!' He's quite entertainin come an huv a wee look, Shug..."

Shug felt the timelessness of the present again, like the "Day of the Macaws" in Burundi when he was placed firmly at the crux of a happening, an awakening; he thought he had been awake since then but realized he had fell into slumber again, seeking the seren-

[31]

ity rather than seeking real being, living to relax rather than relaxing through the changes and challenges, learning how to cope, rather than coping with the learning, but awake, awake now...

He went out, the eagle still soaring above in the huge blue and white sky, behind him Sgurr Mic Coinnich, Sgurr Dubh na Da Bheinn, Sgurr na Bnachdaich, the smell of the cleanest heathery breeze clearing his nose, the gentle gargle of the cold mountain stream, the sun showing the curve of the swelling heavy sea away in the distance.

He had visions of trees sprouting, climbing into the wonderful shapes and colours binding the land...children and fathers and mothers and teenagers in colourful plaid, dancing and singing,working and creating, healthy and free and loving all around him, spinning, taking his hand. It was becoming too strong for him...he cried out in a huge booming voice, "Angus Og! Angus Og!"

Below, Alistair McCloud stopped and turned, looking up to Shug, Tam sitting on a rock, looking a wee bit worried and checking his pockets for change...might need a wee bevy here, he thought.

Shug continued..."Angus Og, Tam McLaverty, we are gathered here tae unite, dream and aspire, we came to this island before, many years ago, I was six foot three in those days, Tam you were just wee bit smaller, a poet and seer, Angus, you fed us salmon and venison, oats and whiskey, we prayed, we said we would travel to the Sassenach city of the Angle to teach them the ways of the earth and to free the city serfs, we vowed that day, and that day has come, not for parliament, not for chiefs, but for the people, for free thinking, for creating, for awakening. Are ye both with me this day...our only now!?"

"Here we go again," thought Tam, "him and his fucking daftness, would he no leave me alone?"

One week later, near Trafalgar Square, London.
Alistair reverse-parked the Highlands and Islands Mobile Library
van into a space, while Tam was singing out the window ,"Were
on the march wi Ally's Army!"

Alistair had thoroughly enjoyed the drive. He would often
disappear for a few days, so the police wouldn't be bothered yet,
anyway. Sergeant McCloud was very busy with case of the disap-
pearing sheep, almost a thousand in the last month; he wouldn't
solve it till he searched every crofter's bedroom and found them
stuffed with live animals, waiting to mysteriously reappear after
the insurance payout.

Shug felt an optimistic fearless rush; he wanted to introduce
himself to everyone. He was passing out books to anyone who
came near.

"Mind an bring it back now!" he shouted.

London went about its business as the three comrades made
their way up Charing Cross Road. Tam looked across at Shug, at
his enthusiastic brightness emanating, the innocence of adventure
driving him forward. His smile asked people to wake up and love,
his eyes said we all belong. Alistair smiled like a baby, like he was
being led and cared for.

"But ah'v never had a high without a low," thought Tam, as
he linked arms with his pals and tried to disguise his fearfulness of
separation and meaninglessness.

"Hey, fancy a waffle and a bottle of Harvey's Bristol Cream?"
he enthused. "They complement each other fuckin brilliant."

Although he was dry nearly two years now, that was all the
permission Shug needed.

[34]

EPISODE 3

Lost on the Circle Line

Some detours on the road to enlightenment. How Tam finds Taoism and begins to call himself a "Humble Worker in the Wood Veneer Warehouse of the Lord". Meanwhile, Shug goes inward and underneath, and while in that darkness he meets another soul with a similar accent and taste for whiskey.

Tam had changed since those first exciting days of comradeship and adventure in London. God knows how it happened, but he seemed to benefit from increased self-esteem after doing a temp agency job in a warehouse. His change began by agreeing with his supervisor that a good job was done that day, and many pallets of wood veneer had indeed been shifted.

Within a couple of weeks he had started showing up sober for work on Monday mornings. One week, he made a sandwich and brought it to work! He always seemed to have some food in the house; he would share with Shug, but did get quite upset when Shug took to stealing sausages in the middle of the night, not so much for the loss of sausage, but more by his failure to live by the "Unified Theory of How to Participate in the World" that they used to follow.

Next thing, taking Shug completely by surprise, Tam said he was moving to a flat in Walthamstow, a real flat. He had a deposit and was happy to stick at his work. His actual words were, "I'll work when ah'm working and all sleep when ah'm…eh, well after work anyway…and if ah'm hungry ill make a wee snack, yummy." How much of this was to do with watching a Winnie the Pooh video while tripping he would never know.

[37]

Well, who knows what our true path is, thought Shug, and congratulated Tam, though he kind of expected that his obsession with wood veneer would wane, and that the comfort of a proper bed and a bookcase to show off his Bird Books and his weighty *A Veneers Companion* would soon become apparent to Tam as being an illusionary distraction.

Tam revelled in the monotony however and felt that he had at last found the hole that he fitted into, slotted in nicely,pre-drilled and safe.

For some weeks Shug would visit occasionally, and often Tam would return home from work to find Shug still sleeping on the couch, some empty cans of out-of-date super-strength lager beside him, and Tam's cigarettes smoked and discarded around the recycling ashtray.

What settled things for Tam was his sadness at hearing Shug tell the same story repeatedly over an evening and then become enraged when he felt the meaning of what he was saying was not being understood nor appreciated. Tam didn't like being scared.

Standing out in the street outside Tam's flat one night, Shug screamed abuse at the neighbours. "Ma brother will come down here and semtex the fuckin lot of ye," he yelled, and "Wake up, wake up ya stupid suburban bastards."

It saddened and scared Shug a lot to hear Tam tell him what he had been doing the previous night. But then, after taking some more from Tam's loose change jar and having a few more cans, he felt indignant, and righteous. He decided to leave Tam a poem, showing him how he had lost a great friend and wise companion.

Scrawled on the back of a brown giro envelope he wrote:

Aye,and off ah go ma freen
And hear no more the warble

Nor the gentle whistling song
Of your Glaswegian soul brother.
Aye, and off ah go ma freen
You fuckin look down on me and ah'll waste ye
Get tae fuck
Shug.

It was to be a while before they were ready to be soulmates again.

Shug and Alistair still lived together at no 17 Pembury, Block 3, Ashurst Estate Hackney. Since Alistair (aka Angus Og) had been barred from being in the sitting room/Shug's bedroom, Shug had been less troubled by Alistair's frequent bottle-breaking, repeated playing of Pink Floyd tracks, and his very scary, childlike talking in his sleep. Alistair was remarkably compliant with the enforced rule that he now sleep in the hallway and was admitted to Shug's room only if intending to buy, or already have purchased and be willing to share, alcoholic beverage. Alistair had discovered a new drug though, and was quite content with living in the hallway.

There was a portable gas cooker (one ring), almost constant electricity, interrupted occasionally by a desperate fuse-thieving exercise carried out usually by Johnny and Linda upstairs, and a Social Security Benefits system that had no interest in appropriate payments and the possible working status of applicants. (Wearing cement and paint-splattered overalls while signing on was frowned upon, but did not in itself warrant further investigation.)

Shug had been pursuing non-attachment to outcomes and a loss of the pressure of expectations; he was getting impatient with it though, and often developed complicated justifications for his egocentric indulgence and need for immediate gratification. Somebody said there was no short cut to serenity and Shug was spending a few years learning this.

His biggest challenge in regard to this calm enlightenment was the "Night before the Giro was Due".

Horror scenarios whizzed round his head. What if the postman threw the letter under the door outside in the hall? It would be stolen. Maybe it wasn't sent out and was lying in a corner of the DSS office, a doc martin footprint on it, discarded, his precious green sheet with his name on it. Maybe this was only Tuesday?

He would lie awake thinking of the fry-up he would be having the next morning after going to the post office and exchanging the magic cheque for real cash, cash that carried so much potential.

He thought about how he would then buy some real tobacco, twenty-five grammes at least, which was bound to last him the two weeks, surely to God.

If he were feeling particularly rejuvenated, spiritual, or optimistic, he would go the market and buy some very cheap socks.

And the money left, it was his, free to go to any bar, off-sales, free to start an adventure. Not clinging to its possible outcome, but relaxed and accepting and at peace, for at least two hours every second Wednesday afternoon.

Today Shug was feeling sorry for himself. From bar to bar and squat to squat he had roamed without finding anyone wanting to get wrecked with him. He ended up sitting for hours at a bus stop, sipping away at his cans, watching the world get on and off buses, an outsider again. Even in this state of isolation, part of Shug believed he was a rock of sanity in a sea of madness, his ego going to great lengths to defend itself and justify his current demise.

He also felt that being so sad and lonesome, broken and incapable, he would be irresistible, and at last would be found by the woman that was meant to love him, whoever she was.

A discarded three-zone travel card came into focus between his feet as he looked down from the bus stop bench.

There was a glow around it…like it was an apparition. Was this a learning task for him? Was he recognising a gateway to synchronistic happenings? It was hard to hear God when this pissed.

Leaning forward to pick it up, Shug fell forward off the bench. He got up again, gallus as an Italian footballer, like it was a common hazard, and a cool enough thing to do.

A number thirty rounded the corner, and he decided to actually get on it rather than just watch.

It was a delight to flash a travel card. Usually he would be sitting upstairs without a ticket, seeing how far he could get before the conductor saw him; this time the sense of being a legitimate traveller was comforting, and good for his esteem and sense of togetherness with all the people on the bus.

He had a gulp of his Super T, such a chemical taste, but there was no doubting its efficiency.

There was a couple in the seat before him, smart but casual, *Time Out* magazine being shared between them.

Shug leaned forward from behind them, wanting to share his sense of togetherness. "Any good bands on tonight? "

The guy turned around, giving a glance to his girlfriend as he did so that seemed to Shug to suggest that he felt Shug was a useless Scottish waster and had no right talking to a stranger, that he was cooler smarter and more handsome, that he would deal with Shug in a mature but superior manner. All in that wee glance.

"Not looking at the music section mate. You'll get one in the newsagent."

"Aw aye," Shug replied. "No bother, might get wan right enough."

He leaned back and had another sip as the couple continued being themselves.

[41]

Shug liked the look of his girlfriend, so English looking, light brown hair and smooth complexion, a donkey jacket and a pink scarf, someone who would be so socialist minded she couldn't fail to fall for Shug in his Troubled Celtic Proletarian Shape.

Shug leaned forward again. "Eh…sorry pal, jist ah noticed the poetry readin there, in support of Nicaragua…where's that oan? Poems reveal what's true but hard to see? Ye no think?"

He smiled at the woman…

"Listen, we're busy…could you leave us alone?" The guy was clearly annoyed.

"Sure…just sayin…poems, ye know?"

There was a short silence until Shug began again.

"In fact ah will just sit back here and recite wan to ye, don't need to listen if you don't want. Its called 'The Bus'.

The smell of a bus is a wonderful thing,
seats and diesel, metal and cleaning product.
Makes me miss maself when ah was young
sittin beside ma maw and da
excited by the winding stairs,
the view from the front
lookin down the periscope.
But now
some bastard sitting there
fuckin wonderin whit to dae
and whit culture to taste
with his fuckin easy money
upsettin ma vibe,
killin ma communication.

As Shug made up and recited his poem the couple got their bag and walked down stairs, so he had to shout his words until the hard looks of a few old women silenced him.

Looking out the window he could see Angel Islington station up ahead and decided to have a wander inside.

Before heading to the tube, Shug remembered there was a Marks and Spencer's round the corner that was fairly easy to steal from. His too big jacket with its torn lining was ideal, his confidence levels were high, and he could still walk without bumping into things. Conditions were perfect.

(Most clothes didn't fit Shug. Somehow he was the wrong size, small was too small and medium too big. He had long arms, short legs, slight chest, strong shoulders and small feet. With his long blonde hair and blue eyes he felt he should have been a bit more Germanic in stature, but three generations of slumping and sausages had created his more Scottish mongrel shape, a shape that suited itself nicely to random charity-shop couture.)

He would buy something of course, maybe a bar of chocolate. He walked into the store, trying to look like he was in need of a bar of Cadbury's and nothing else, oh no, just the one thing on my mind, can't you see? I'm a chocolate kinda guy.

He wandered down the off-sales isle anyway, just to have a wee look at the drink he might buy for a dinner party sometime. After glancing around he slips a bottle of Bell's into his big pocket... phew, a wee walk around, not too much, bar of Cadbury's in hand and his jacket bunched together in front, casual like. Twenty five pence? No problem. Here, got it exactly. Keep walking, don't look round, out the door and down the busy street, quickly, holding the chocolate bar aloft. Hey, I bought chocolate, see? Man, the nerves but, need a drink...lucky me, I have one here...

Shug went down an alley of the market street and screwed open the bottle top, a nice strong fume, a hint of peaty mountain water, gulping down its heat, ahhh, my companion for today, pleased to meet you.

He started off for the tube station, but buoyed by his success with the whiskey he decided he wanted a nice book to carry on his travels, and possibly read one sober week; a great way to get rid of time, reading.

The bookshop had its doors open to the pavement and the shopkeeper seemed really interested in books and was actually reading one; well, didn't seem too difficult.

Since Alistair had sold the Highlands and Islands Mobile Library to some travellers, his supply of free reading had gone. It happened so quickly there was no time to start unloading the philosophy section. The buyer, sensing they were in not a very strong position, haggled then down from five hundred pounds to two hundred and ten pounds. It was a shameful act that had now deprived many isolated crofters of their weekly arrears visit. But still, two hundred pounds, can't argue with that.

Shug realized he was browsing in the childbirth and women's health section. Now what am I looking for...spirituality and mysticism maybe,

Shape-shifting Made Easy...nah, fuckin scary.

Purple or Pink? A Guide to Your Unseen Vibrational Colour...mibbe, but ah'm pretty sure its green already.

Food as Spirituality: the Dynamics of Making Healthy Choices...I know ah'm evil, pies are evil.

Maintaining his open-mindedness, Shug saw a thick green book with some Celtic patterns. Looking good...what's this then?

Knowing: the Lies, the Limitations and the Randomness of Human Perception Exposed...That's the very man for me... sounds fuckin clever enough anyway, he thought. Shug glanced though a few pages before kneeling down and quietly slipping it into his jacket lining. A gentle splash may have been audible, but...no problem, nobody looking. A quick look at a huge children's atlas near the door and out, a free man with a book, a travel card, whiskey and a few pounds. "Yes," thought Shug, "let the day unfold."

"Hey, comrade, how far can ah go wi this three-zone card?" Shug asked at the ticket desk.

"How far?" The elderly Jamaican gentleman smiled.

"Ha, you want to go as far as you can, eh? Well, I suggest the Circle Line, my friend. You just keep on goin round, ha ha, I'm sure you'll travel pretty far. Get your moneys worth, ha ha."

Not a bad idea, thought Shug.

The escalators always seemed so much like an instrument of the state, shifting people around in their unawareness. Shug wondered if he could remember every face he saw going past him on the other side, storing them on his hard drive for some reason not yet known of. "Maybe there's a memory test when ye die," Shug pondered. "Ye'd never know wi God."

Being the polite and social-minded Glaswegian he was, it took Shug some time to get on the train. Showing up others to be thoughtless and egocentric was a hobby of his, and for a while he took great pride in his refusal to barge his way on. However, three trains later, he revised his methodology and shouted and cursed his way past people, momentarily lapsing in his concern for all sentient beings.

He found a seat and got himself comfortable for the journey; it was 4pm, so if the tube ends at, say 1am, that would be nine hours. A long journey.

Opening his big clever book, he began reading aloud, first smiling around the coach to show he was not mental, just clever. Holding his chin in his hand he turned a few pages, slowly and drunkenly, and nodded to himself "...should all experienced experience be discounted due to the possibility of limited sensory capability? Do we create our own view of life, and consequently our own experiences through intention?

"What do ye think, big man? "Shug asked the person opposite.

The train became louder as it braked and pulled into King's Cross station. The man got up and before leaving the train took a leaflet from his briefcase and gave it to Shug: *The Pentecostal Church of Later day Saints.*

"This is what I think"

"Oh, ah should ah known I'd pick some religious nut tae talk tae eh?"

Settling back in his seat, Shug became quiet; he closed the book and closed his eyes, spent some time thinking about the guy who looked at him in a shoe shop ten years ago, like he was looking down his nose because he was trying on cheap trainers.

"Bastard!" Shug shouted at this memory.

The African looking woman next to him looked over her glasses at Shug, and spent a good second studying him.

"Hows it gawn?" asked Shug.

"No bad at aw" she replied, laughing,

"Where ye fae? "

"Ambollo Gola…hey, nice talkin but ah need tae get aff here… aw the best son…C'mon the Macaws!"

Then she was gone, out into Warren Street station, leaving Shug wondering how to explain the significance of his encounter there to the strangers around him. He decided not to bother, being somewhat confused about it himself.

Next thing, taking Shug completely by surprise, the elbow of the woman on the other side of him gently pressed against his. She was wearing jeans, a black t-shirt and a combat jacket. Short dark hair, her reflection in the carriage window made him insane. It was about thirty seconds now and she still hadn't pulled her elbow away. He was in love.

He tried hard not to move, but was lurched forward by a sideways shuggle of the train, accidently brushing her book with his arm.

"Sorry…knocked yer book there…just when we were gettin on so well, eh?"

She smiled. "It's okay."

Shug tried hard to remember what Tam used to say about first meetings, something about ninety percent of communication being non-verbal.

He tried hard not to talk, but instead stretched his arms out in front of him, turning his hands slowly like he was holding a golden ball of light, spinning one way then the other. He breathed out hard and relaxed his feet, tensing his toes up then letting go. He brought his knees up like a yoga stretch but quickly let them back down when he noticed that his blue and grey odd socks, inside out and ripped at the heel, were visible.

Conversation was difficult on the tube.

"Jist doin ma Tie Kwan Do, ye know."

"Sorry?"

"Ma exercises, ah'm no gonny be fuckin aw undergrun an feart an that, ah'm part of the earth an feelin the energy of the core, e'r felt the energy of ra core?"

"I'm not sure eh, check the map." She pointed to the colourful squiggles on the carriage wall, hoping that was a relevant answer.

"Yeah, beautiful, your right! Like, aw weavin in an oot? Criss crossin. Colours and waves…ya wee dancer!" He started making wave shapes with his hands and arms.

"Ye know, I think we're in tune me an you. Whit dae ye dae? Naw let me guess, yer a researcher for Amnesty International? Ah love aw that by the way. Who's torturin who, mental. Ah remember a wee sayin there, 'It isnae those that inflict the most but those that endure the most that will conquer' but ah think that's a load a pish, cos everything happens now, always now, no winners an losers at the end ye know?"

She smiled. With the noise of the rattling train she failed to understand any of Shug's chat, but somehow she recognised him, his reaching out, sharing, his interest in the world or something. So when he asked for a pen and wrote his name on a page he tore from his book she took it politely. "Shug, Flat 17 Pembury Block 3, Hackney" it said, and "Write to me when your drunk. Elbows of the world unite!"

Once home, Sharon read the torn-off page: "If you see something different from me, from a different angle, distance etc, and that thing is no-thing but a wave, and you too are no-thing but a wave, then feel the wave, trust, vibrate at your true frequency... influence other waves."

"Yeah," she thought, "might be something in it."

After that encounter Shug fell into a sleep that cleared the seats around.

The train eventually came to rest at King's Cross station.

"Hey, Mister, you can't sleep here, time to go home. Up you get, man, now off you go. The escalator is over there. Off you go, man"

Shug shifted, and sleep-walked his way off the train, obeying the worker's commands until he got to the escalator, which he walked past and went into a storeroom that had been left unlocked. Curling up under a table in the dark, he resumed his slumber.

Like many events in his life there was no planning, only the prioritising of the 'easier, softer way' as he made his way through life's obstacles.

[48]

Dreaming was often an interchange between his drunken subconscious and his drunken conscious. Sensory experience became thought, thought became physical. As he lay there kicking his feet against the table legs, his mind carried his ego to Hampden Park, Glasgow, and a penalty shoot-out. He was wearing a dufflecoat and drinking a bottle of American Cream Soda as he stepped up to take his kick. The goalkeeper was Bruce Forsyth and it was Scotland versus England...but he had to remember something before he was allowed to shoot...a clock alarm radio, a large cuddly bear, a toaster, a set of matching...what? A set of matching fucking what? What the fuck was it? Scotland would lose, Scotland would lose...

"Candle holders! Ya Beauty!" he shouted as he kicked his leg out and battered his shin on the hard wooden edge, sending Bruce the wrong way and...

"Oh fuck...aww!" The pain spread from his leg, wakening him as it travelled up to his head. He wasn't sure where he was. The kitchen? Tam's? Hampden Park?

Different bits of his head started communicating with each other and the jigsaw became clearer; he was still in the underground, it was late, he had a little whiskey left, he had tobacco, he was cold, he had a very sore leg.

Only emergency lights illuminated the platform as he crawled out of the store-room. As he walked along the platform a cold dread crept up on him; trying not to be aware of it, he made his way to the escalators and started walking up. Whatever the miscalculation that people make when they get on a stationary escalator, it is usually slight and quickly readjusted. Shug, however, overreacted big time; he kicked the step in front then tried to jump backwards but instead toppled forwards, battering his forehead, just above the nose, directly on the edge of a higher step. He nearly fainted at the pain, the wetness of blood trickling down his face; in panic he made his way up.

"Got tae get out of here, man, this is getting bad, this is wrong, Shug." He made it to the top but the shutters were down and he could go no further. He started banging on the metal.

"Hoy, hello! Hello there! Ah'm stuck in here."

He listened but could hear nothing.

"Hello! Security! Wake up, man, down here! Let us out! Ah'm stuck here man."

Shug slumped down and rolled a cigarette. If he got out it would be fine, he would walk to the fish and chip shop on Seven Sisters road, get a couple of cans, some chips even, head home to bed, another wee adventure, eh…be funny telling people, the bold Shug, chaos and bad choices.

He took out the bottle of whiskey, about a third left, and had a gulp, feeling the heat burn down his throat.

The last time he felt this bad, this lost, was in the African rainforest; he remembered his longing for his parents and God to make things all right.

"And what did I do? I kept going, man, took some action, and help was there, Big Ade, eh?" He hadn't heard from Big Ade Adeyobo since that last scribbled drunken letter, something about being in jail for attacking a group of workers from a logging company, team-handed with a fleeto of macaws.

After banging the metal shutters a while more, a panic took hold of him again and he ran off down the escalators,

"Need to get out, need to get out, what if I have a heart attack, or fit, fuck's sake? Ah need to get out of here."

Looking down through the tunnel Shug heard a faint crack and thud noise, quite far off. It was pitch black down there. How far to the Angel from Kings Cross? Well, it didn't look far on the squiggly map anyway, half a mile? Half a mile and he might get out, get some cans, come out of the darkness under London showing how brave he was. He was no sheep getting carried about on a escalator, he was a free man!

And smashed to pulp by an oncoming train? Grated and sliced along the metal track?

There were no trains though, not for hours surely. Why was he stuck down a tube station? Surely a mystical challenge? To find one's way out of the depths, and after a few cans never, ever, drink again? Is that the message, God?

"Well I might just fuckin do it," he exclaimed to the empty station.

He sat at the edge of the platform; there were definitely some kind of noises coming from inside the tunnel. He eased himself down on to the track,

"Fuck," he thought, "is it electric? Surely they unplug it at night…" Stepping from sleeper to sleeper he made his way along, feeling the curved edge of the tunnel. Shaking with the cold, he took another swig of whiskey and made a roll-up with some difficulty in the dark.

Show me the way to go home,
I'm tired and I want to go to bed,
I had a little drink about an hour ago
and it went right to my head.

Nothing like a song to keep you going.

It was dark both ways now that he had gone a few hundred yards out of the station. He noticed some small side tunnels along the way, good for jumping out the way of an approaching train, he figured, if luck was on his side.

He remembered that a few years ago hundreds of Scottish football fans had got out of a broken-down tube train and walked through the tunnel to Wembley Stadium. Stirred with pride, he marched on.

Were on the march wi Ally's Army,
we're going to the Argentine
and we'll really shake them up
when we win the world cup
cos Scotland are the greatest football team!

Half a mile away down the tunnel, Johnny (Elvis) Docherty was dressed in white overalls with an oxygen mask on his face and sweat pouring from him as he lifted and crashed a pick axe into the asbestos foundation beneath the railway sleepers.

His colleague Eddie Sweeney pushed in his shovel and dug up the rubble, passing it to young Danny Murphy. Danny bagged it and hauled the bag along to a trolley, hoisting the heavy weight on before returning to his position.

John had been working in the tunnels two months now. It was only four hours actual working, and £50 a night. He preferred it to work on a site, at the age of 44 his harsh life had damaged him physically and mentally. Eddie and Danny had been only a couple of nights, but already the strange conditions were taking their toll. There was little talking, mainly due to the masks. The foreman would move down the line shouting, "Move the trolley along now" and "Swap around, lads, there" but time went by pretty slowly, with only the occasional rat-killing to liven things up.

John wasn't feeling right tonight. He had been getting worried about his lack of sleep. Feelings of remorse and loneliness were always with him, and not even the drink could remove them, but the drink kept him stuck, doing nothing about it. And now was he hearing things?

"Kin ye hear that?" he shouted at the two Irishmen.

They gestured with a shrug of the shoulders and a shake of the head. Conditions and accents weren't very conducive to small talk.

After a few moments John put his pick down and, after taking his mask off, shouted again, "There's someone down the track singin the Scotland World Cup song of 78…ye know the wan?"

Eddie smiled. "Eh no. I think I can hear the Fields of Athenry though, what about you Danny?"

"Maybe its The Jam, yeah! Hear it now? Down in the tube station at midnight wooohoooohoo?"

"Oh fuck off."

Eddie tried to reassure him. "Take it easy, Johnny, it's weird being down here, we'd all hear things at times, eh?"

Johnny went back to work, hoisting the pick and crashing it into the concrete floor. London was a bastard, smash! fucking hostels, bosses, publicans, rich smart ass-fuckers, crack!

Shug stood quiet for a moment, having realized the weight of London was above him, ten million sleeping people. Such massive unconsciousness, it was scary. Even the government was asleep, Mrs Thatcher dreaming of stealing bottles of milk from huge cows with miners' hats on.

Some poor bastard dreaming the opposite. Dreams of sex, and dreams of mountaineering, dreams of Blue Peter presenters making atom bombs, dreams of home, and dreams of death, dreams of antelope DJs, so many dreams.

Shug came back to his present. He was in a narrow dark tube, wanting to see the light, but couldn't get out by himself. Was he meant to get out? Did he want to get out? What did he want to be when he got out? The same again? Finding more scenarios of a drunken nature, challenging free choice to confirm its truth? The possibility of bad decisions? He always found that a powerful notion, the divergence from the current moment into all its possible forms, through thought. Through dreams.

He took out his bottle of Bell's, only a gulp left now, his umbilical cord, his cosy womb life juice, ahhh, settling his spirit, warming his soul, connecting him briefly to a safe oneness. But he had still to be born, out of here.

For some reason Shug thought of his father. He hadn't seen him since he was 10, when he was being dragged out the house by the police after smashing the place up, and soon after which he moved down to England. A few drunken calls at Christmas, then nothing. He was an idea in Shug's head, for him to ignore or reinvent at will. He remembered his singing though; at family gatherings the atmosphere was so light and social it felt great, anecdotes and banter flying across the room.

"One singer, one song," his uncle would shout, his bright Donegal eyes smiling like the Buddha's as he laughed.

His dad was always first. He wasn't a great singer but it was one of the few things he really enjoyed. The warmth of his higher-self, the openness and happiness of a usually dour character, made the whole room feel good.

As I was walkin doon the street
ah met wee Johnny Scobie.
Says he tae me, could ye go a hawf
says I, man, that's ma hobby.

Everyone would join in the chorus.

Oh ah'm no awa tae bide awa

ah'm no awa tae lee ye
no ah'm no awa tae bide awa
ah'll ail come back an see ye!

Shug was crying now.

"Didnae come back an see us, did ye?"

Crying was one of a number of side effects of the whiskey-induced emotional turbulence, usually of feeling sorry for one's self variety, or a righteous rage.

He kept on down the track with anger in his step now, quickly following on from the sadness.

"Didnae come back did ye? Oh naw, just leave the boy and his mother in Possil, they'll be fine, eh, fuckin life chances. How many did ye leave us? Gie few, and there aw shite!" His words bounced their way down the tunnel.

Johnny rested his pick for a moment as he felt a tremor run through him; his hands were shaking, his legs weak as his heart began bouncing around to a strange beat inside his chest. He knew he should have taken the medications prescribed to him but, to be honest, he didn't believe there was anything wrong that a drink wouldn't fix…bad nerves, that's all.

He struggled for a breath, panting shallow and light, taking off his mask and bending over.

"Carry on, boys, be with ye in a minute. I'll sit down…Jesus."

Head in hands and scared for his life, he sat there on the track, almost fainting, waves of hot and cold travelling up his neck to his head.

"Ah'm in a right bad situation here," he thought. Things weren't "no bad", things were "bad".

Then the words came at him through the darkness, the twilight zone near hell.

[55]

"Didnae come back…Possil…boy and his mother…bastard… chances? Didnae come back…leave the boy…fuckin life…"

They bounced around his head loud and quiet, near and far.

Eddie and Danny could here it too; they turned their heads towards the noise, their head-torches shining down the tunnel.

Shug saw the two lights and tried to understand them. A ghost train? People? It was people, fucking workers or something. He shouted towards them-

"Hey, how's it gawn! Can you see me? Hey..!"

Johnny stood up as Shug got nearer; this was some bad game going on in the head. Eddie and Danny didn't know whether to run away or run and help.

Carrying a book, and a bottle of whiskey sticking out of his pocket, Shug staggered and limped from sleeper to sleeper, blood from his forehead covering his face. He put his hand in his other pocket and took out the three-zone travel card.

"Got ma ticket here, pal, nae probs!" he shouted, then "The Bold Shug does it again! Is this the Angel?"

John Docherty looked at his son, his wee Shugie, all grown up now, and down a tube tunnel in London at three in the morning, pissed out of his head and bleeding.

Shug Docherty fell forward into his dads arms. How the hell could it be? Is this…ma da?

Both men lost consciousness and crumpled side by side on the tracks. Eddie and Danny hoisted them on to the trolley and made for the station platform, wondering if they would get paid for the whole shift.

EPISODE 4

'If you're proud to be a Buddhist
clap your hand'

Being the Genesis of the Possilpark Paradigm Shift Fleeto (PPSF)

It must have been the twentieth time he had read it that morning. To get any letter that wasn't in a brown envelope with a prepaid stamp was very rare, and he shook as he opened it, tearing it roughly in his hungover impatience.

Sharon McGlade
Dzogchen Beara
Retreat and Meditation Centre
Castletownbere
Co Cork
Ireland

Dear Shug,
I'm not drunk so forgive my indulgence, but I wanted to let you know that sitting beside you on the underground that evening some months ago (perhaps you don't remember, that's okay) was a meaningful moment for me. I had spent that day at an AA convention, yes I'm alcoholic, perhaps that's why I'm taking this risk as I sensed a similar spiritual malady in yourself. Anyway, I was close to drinking that evening, but our brief encounter, and the wise words that were on your note, gave me the little push I needed towards my 'Higher Power' as we say at our meetings. I won't go into details, but I wanted to send this note, to say thanks and I hope all is well with you. Let go and let God.
Sharon.

Somehow, just reading and rereading gave him some solace from panic, and he would pick it up and lay it down every few minutes. *Let go and let God*...but he would float off into an alcoholic fit if he let go...Must focus and click his fingers, feel his tongue, not swallow it...oh hell...who makes his heart beat so fast? Fear swept through him in waves...*let God*...well yes, I will, get me a drink and I'll change, a roll- up and a think, a think with the roll-up, there, phew, oh help, oh faster, fuckin water, a small gulp. Is that bottle empty? It is, it's been empty for...read that again slow, the words, *Hello Shug*. That's beautiful, things are gonny be all right, fuck what have I done, where's Alistair? Sick coughing spasm of the stomach. Alistair is dead. Alistair is dead, he died. He didn't die, he was killed, killed by a truck on the A1 at Archway, sent home to his Island beaten and dead. Ah'm sorry Alistair, ah'm sorry, ah'm fuckin sorry, and times up for me too times up for me. He picked up the letter again.

To recall memories, how to do it, where are they? That drunken night in the underground...the tunnel he remembered okay, how could he forget the most meaningful moment in his life? But Sharon? A note? Wisdom?

Not unusual for him to chat with someone, but they listened and wrote to me? AA? Is that how they operate maybe, target wasters like me, make up stories, the bastards.

He dug his hand back into the upturned couch, feeling for coins; maybe he had missed something, twenty seven pence he had, cheapest can was 80p, leaves 53p, must be, somewhere...or maybe I'll go to the shop, lost a pound I'll say, dropped it, just wanted some margarine, oh and a can there, Tenants please? Give it back when I come back down is that okay? Yeah, it's been weeks since I borrowed there, thank God for my prudent use of Ali's General Convenience Store.

After procuring the can Shug wandered around hoping to meet someone who was wandering around looking for someone to drink with. He was meeting his dad later, first time since getting out of hospital. In the three days there they had talked little. Shug was in general medical with concussion and a fractured shin, and his dad in cardiology for an Angiogram and an opener for one of his arteries, clogged by the cravings of the unenlightened mind.

His thoughts kept coming back to that letter, *Wisdom, AA, Sharon*. He had stopped drinking through spiritual experiences a few times before. Tam had come to recognize when one of these episodes was approaching and tapped him for a few pound just at the right moment. Alistair had tried to help Shug directly, quoting reference upon reference, a bibliography of sources, he said. "You have a disease, Shug – *WHO Report on Alcohol Use*, pp. 136-139, you have a genetic predisposition, Shug – *Addiction Studies/ Familial Histories*, Hesseldorf, G, pp 27-45. You're a beer-monster, Shug – Angus Og, just noo, speaking." He said it often, usually while his mellow heroin-calmed head saw hope for others but not for itself; wisdom for others, ignorance for Alistair. Ignorance and then death.

Still, *ground luminosity*, the *bardo of becoming*, that's the story for Angus now.

"What's the story, Angus?"

"The story of becoming again, Shug, *let go and let God.*"

And what the fuck was Dzogchen Beara?

***

Tam sat in his orange robes, eating an egg sandwich in the works canteen. He was top veneer selector in the warehouse now. Turning a whole log of veneer was an art to him. He could sense a "door panel" or a "pearl small table" before he had even seen it. He marvelled at a whole crown, delighting in its symmetry; he could read a crown of wood like a poem, feeling the trees life, the warm summers, children climbing on the lower branches, the shock of a lightening storm, its memory curved and shaped into its heart. He was also fast. Like a Chinese Wai- Lai master, he lifted and turned the batch, smoothly showing prospective buyers the nature of the wood. Placing the sheaves on the new palate was intuitive perfection; to be his partner in the turning was to share in an effortless and natural swinging dance.

But some said he had taken things too far. His wisdom of things, his ability to classify and recognize, did not help in his relationships with people or with himself.

There was a loneliness that sometimes felt like he could not have empathy with anyone. He felt like he was wondering through everyone else's world, an observer but not a player. In the staff canteen, sitting at his own table, he was mocked by the loud young men that weren't looking for any answers because they weren't asking any questions. They expected something different from Tam, a laugh, a wild joker with attitude, an aggressively opinionated but companionable Glaswegian, something, but not a spiritual seeker.

At home, after his work, was the hardest time for Tam. He spent his evening cooking,talking to himself, reading, or listening to meditative chants. He chanted himself sometimes, his guttural sounds could be mistaken for a Tibetans, but instead of "Om mane pad me hum" his sounded like "Oh Mammy take me hame" And that was a more meaningful statement for him.

But his mammy wasn't there to take him home. And Alistair wasn't there. Bless the air he breathed. And Shug wasn't there, Shugworthy, the bold Shugie Docherty, his companion of the earth realm, schemie pal, and spiritual brother, wasn't there. And he felt unwell. And he wanted to get away from his unwellness.

He took a wander outside, down on to Walthamstowe High Street. He stood outside Woolworths, watching people pass by. Losing his focus was dangerous; a regular, ordered day kept Tam at peace. What was he looking for here? Buses came and went, cars stopped and moved off again, people looked in windows or walked into shops.

Like a daydream he went walking, not knowing where he was going, his green parker zipped up high over his bright robes, head down as he shuffled like an octogenarian monk up the high street towards Hackney.

Overhead, a seagull called and called and seemed to guide Tam forward. He would look up occasionally and it would be looking down at him.

"Ahh eeek ahhh ekkkk ah eeeeky," it would screech, which Tam knew meant "'This way, this way, go this way." It had a fairly strong east-end accent, but he could still make it out.

He crossed the river up towards Clapton, and the gull swerved down and to the right along the water. "Ahh eeek," it screeched again as it flew off, its job done.

The river and marshes around were bordered by pylons and a railway line, a brief gap of earth and vegetation, mainly inhabited by butterflies, mice, tadpoles, and people who either rode bikes, or shouted at dogs.

Tam sat at the edge of the river, watching the water flow. A family of ducks came over, but Tam had no food to give them, only advice. "Quack...quack quack quack...qua...qua quack," he implored.

His thinking became more and more disjointed as his ordered routine crumbled.

There was a fusion of himself and his environment, but it didn't seem healthy, holistic; it felt like he couldn't direct his thinking. He wasn't part of a wise and loving universe, like in his meditations. He was not just losing his ego, he was losing his true frequency, he was not tuned in, all waves around him were distorted and buckled as they entered his energy.

And part of him knew this and part of him was scared, but at present it was a very weak part.

Behind him and overlooking the river was a small block of council flats. An arrhythmic beat boomed out from an open window. "Ja rastafari ja ja ja rastafari ja ja rast a ja ja rasta the city too hot, I man go to the country, the city too hot I man better go now, up to the mountains, the city too hot, I man need to cool down, upon the mountain top."

This sounded good. Tam turned and looked up and shouted to the window, "Yeah, brother, the city too hot!"

A black man of about 50 with dreadlocks, a torn black t-shirt and a gappy smile was at the window, looking like he'd survived quite a few altered states of mind in his time.

"You wanna smoke, bro? Come up, come round the front, yeah. I an I open the door for you, scotty."

Tam made his way round and was let in, the music still loud, and the beat seemed almost visible.

The air was heavy with grass smoke.

"I give you a little taste...what's your name, friend? I and I is Malcolm, Malcolm the Punk they call me, for I is a sex pistol pteeeew! ha ha! I is high and I is dry"

He poured a drink from a bottle of brandy.

"The city too hot, I man have to cool down upon the mountain." Singing, he began joining papers together.

"Ma names Tam McLaverty, from the parish of Possil in the

[62]

heart of the Dear Green Place." Tam felt like someone else was talking.

"Welcome, Tam, from the Dear Green Place."

Tam hadn't smoked in over a year, since he first started settling down at work. Still, he sometimes felt distortions in colour and sound even without a smoke, even voices at times. It was a bit annoying, but given his heavy ingestion of mushrooms and acid over the years he felt it was not unusual to have been slightly damaged. And so far the voices were supportive, if slightly uncontrollable.

He hadn't seen a doctor since moving to London, in fact he didn't have a doctor, and it was about three years since being on any psychiatric medication, even when he was on it he was on so much other stuff too he never knew if it was working.

Malcolm passed the lighted joint and Tam automatically took it. He sucked hard and felt a hot blast go down into his lungs, a very sweet-grass smokiness. He held his breath then exhaled. Immediately he felt his heart quicken. He took a few more draws and passed it back.

"Nice, man, nice," said Malcolm, relaxed on the couch opposite.

As Tam sat there his fragile grip on reality loosened even further.

Malcolm became very threatening, like he was shouting at Tam. But he was only singing.

The music vibrated through him – boom boom, Babylon burning, boom boom, Babylon gonny fall, boom boom, all the birds are singing, boom boom, all the words are minging, boom boom, heavy metal twinging, boom boom, ping pong all wrong pass the bong, boom boom, how long Tam been gone, how long to sing along, sing along supporter, up the Celts, feel the belts…

He got up to get out but Malcolm was saying something about

money and had his hand on his shoulder. Tam felt his close presence was like a searing pain in his head, he pushed him back and ran.

He ran and ran terrified, blindly, bouncing off the wall of the alleyway that went back to the river walk. His parker seemed to weigh him down so he tore it off and threw it in the river. He got quite away from Malcolm who was shouting after him.

"Hey! Take it easy, man, I and I is saying about your robes man, how cool is your robes man, Rastafari! You is gone, my friend."

Tam ran and ran and ran straight into a riverside pub he'd been in before with Shug, well known for its extra-strength beer. Tam gasped for breath at the counter. "Extra...strength...beer "

A few recognizable faces watched him from the tables around the bar, saying things to hurt him.

"Joined the Krishna, ya nut?"

"C'mon...c'mon...hurry up Hari, c'mon!"

"Hey, the Holy Jock! Suppose your looking for alms..."

All the horrible faces laughing, big hateful eyes, ugly sharp black and yellow teeth, greyness and smoke. The whole pub, screaming contorted features. Tam's skin began to feel so hot, hot and sore, covered in sores, stinging, he grabbed the pint on the counter and poured it over his head, his red hair dripping, his robes soaked, but cooler, cooler, he ran out to get away from this Tribe of Idiots, the Wednesday Afternoon Devils.

The walkway opened up to become a park, at last some space. He stopped running and walked up a steep grassy hill. The plants were alive, but harsh, sharp, dangerous; he bent to pull up some nettles, feeling the stings, brushing the leaves across his face, screaming but feeling, at least feeling.

He stuffed plants down the front of his robe, nettles, weeds, grass. He put grass on his head, he dug into the earth and rubbed mud over his face A bright yellow and gold butterfly flew up in front of him and he gave chase, wanting to eat it, feel its juices, its papery lightness. "Like holy communion," he thought. He grabbed it and trapped it between his hands.

"Holy, Holy, Holy God of power and might, heaven and earth are full of your glory, hosanna in the highest. Lord, I am not worthy to receive you, but only say the word and I shall be healed."

Tam lifted his hands and took the butterfly in his mouth, felt it fluttering inside. He puffed out his cheeks to let it fly, tickling his palate and lips. Mustn't bite, he thought, let it dissolve. Kneeling, he bowed his head. Slowly the creatures spasms stopped; Tam chewed its thin stickiness. Amen.

As he raised his head and opened his eyes five Hasidic Jews were around him and watching, all in black long coats, curly hair falling from black high hats.

They quickly dispersed as he got up and started shouting "Get out of the temple!" He ran around trying to catch one of them.

"Eat grass and follow me!…No hats! For God has spoke of this! … Babylon a fall down. Ja Rastafari…you are ma chosen people…and you and you and every last wan of us, and me, and no-me, and no-body and no-thing…"

When at last the police and doctor found Tam, he was sitting in the goldfish pond in the park greenhouse in lotus position, with fish swimming around him and a palm leaf on his head, an expression of total tight-lipped fear on his face, masquerading as blissful contentment.

There was no struggle as they took him off in an ambulance to Homerton Hospital. A tiny part of him knew that was where he needed to be.

★★★

Shug met with his dad that night in the Dolphin Bar. His dad lived in a nearby hostel, and had done so for twelve years. Resettlement workers came and went but Johnny Elvis was staying put. He worked, he smoked, he drank, he read the paper, put on a couple of bets each day, and sang Elvis songs at the local pub at the Sunday free talent night.

He coped as best he could with his regrets and with his shame and isolation. In the hostel, he occasionally flared up at the staff, usually when some new young worker would ask him lots of questions again, and treat him like a lesser being, through professional kindness.

Sharing meals with a group of other men saddened him; he would have a decent chat at times with the cook, or with some staff, or with a barmaid, but they were on the other side of the counter, always a counter.

His cubicle of a room was just a place to sleep. Every morning he was up and out to work or to spend the hours drinking a little, gambling a little, and perhaps spend some time in the library.

He had thought of returning to Glasgow, but had developed an ingrained chronic resentment to his wife. Anyway, here he was, unexpectedly thrown into a familial reunion. Shug was fairly difficult when young. He remembered a number of incidents. The time he went on to the altar and spent the whole mass playing with Lego figures. "Holy Jesus take that, pow! Hey, I'm too good for you, devil man, splat!" He was escorted off and dropped his figures, shouting "I want my Jesus back!" to the amusement of the congregation. Somehow though, he seemed profound in his innocence.

Or the time he ran away with the wee boy McLaverty, built a den, and painted on it "You are now entering Free Weansville". Quite a struggle they put up too when it was being knocked down and the boys evicted. The boy's mother was mad on him though and Shugie could do no wrong. She understood the existential angst he was suffering. She struggled too with the confusion of life in Possil; there was more than this, and she knew she was out of place.

Sometimes when they were getting on fine, she would recount to him her dreams, tales of horses in the Gobi desert and mystical mountains. While serving food in the local Chinese restaurant, she would expound her wisdom to all the customers. She would talk in her sleep too. She upset John when she quoted Kahlil Gilbran at him: "These are not your children, they are the children of life, they come through you but are not from you"

Shug had managed to find a little money during the day. It wasn't the plastic bag full of notes that he tried so hard to visualize into existence, but a loan from a friend – well, used to be friend, now money lender and reflection of Shug's crumbling self-esteem – so he was already fairly steamed when his dad came in; nothing like the excuse of an important event to allow you to get drunk.

He had got there early and was spending his time building up a character through the juke box. An hour later he was a lonely cowboy, a love 'em and leave 'em biker, an angst-filled art student, and an Irish republican soldier – in fact, typical Dolphin Bar clientele.

"Dad, howdy man, good to see ye, what will ah get ye?"

John was a short stocky man, with fast eyes, very mobile eyebrows, and a rough red face, suspicious, but quick to relax when he felt no threat. A fair man in general, but sometimes his defensiveness closed him off to any understanding, beyond what he already felt he knew.

"Well thanks, son, I'll have a lager and a wee wan."

Shug felt proud as he ordered the drinks, him and his dad, refugees, the estranged father, the prodigal son. In London, mystically reunited through the collision of atoms in that particle accelerator called the Circle Line.

"Ye sure now, Dad, how's the old ticker?"

"Fine son…takin ma tablets"

They sat down in the corner. Shug felt his dad was sitting too far away, John felt his son was too near. They kind of unconsciously compromised.

They sat silently for a while. John took a good gulp of lager and followed it with a sip of whiskey, a sense of homage on his face to the golden spirit. In the background Christy Moore sang "Ordinary Man".

What was meant to happen here? Neither really knew, perhaps just a bit of catching up.

"So…you been working down the tunnels long, Dad? That's a dark hell of a place eh?"

"Bad enough, aye, but just a few hours a night, gives us more time during the day to do ma stuff."

"What stuff's that?"

"Well, odds an ends, getting by ye know." His eyes darted uncomfortably at the attention on himself.

"And whit about yerself now, son? Does your mother know yer wanderin about drunk in the underground system? Christ sake, boy, what ye playin at?"

"Ye don't get tae tell me off, Da, ye've nae right anymare, okay? Mam knows ah'm here right enough, told her ah was involved in the BBC, studio sets an that"

"An are ye?"

"Well, I was there wan day shuntin furniture aboot in the basement, but need to make her feel okay, ye know? She worries…"

Shug looked across at his dad. When he was younger he looked up to his dad like he was Billy Bremner, the Scotland midfield dynamo. As he watched the World cup in Germany 1974, his dad and his pals taking on the mighty Brazil, carrying his hopes, showing him pride, strong and in control of the match, and then...missing a sitter that would have given Scotland victory...Dad how could you miss, how could you let me down?

Johnny pointed at Shug's drink. "Whits that?"

"Snakebite and blackcurrant."

"Fuck off, ah'm no askin for that here."

He handed a fifty pound note over to Shug.

"Get it out of that an keep the change."

"Eh, thanks Dad." For a drinker it didn't take much to get a feeling of temporary forgiveness and bonhomie. Just money for drink, that's all.

Shug went up to the counter, got the drinks, and put some coins in the juke box. He thought he was okay, just a bit merry, but he had got into that emotional blackout state, where he would be buffeted around by transient emotions and spurred into actions that wouldn't be remembered, by fleeting notions blown up into important *do or die, now or never, all or nothing, who do you think I am?* scenarios.

He returned with the drinks to the sound of "The Hills of Donegal" behind him.

"Still follow the Celtic, Dad?"

"Ah read the papers, son. Not doin too bad, eh? Ever go and see them? Wi that pal of yours, whits his name, Tommy McLaverty?"

"Tam, aye, not for a few years now tho. Tam's down here too but ah don't see him much, went a bit kinda quiet an funny, in on himself, ye know?"

"He had funny eyes that boy, look right through ye. So eh, what else you been up to? No woman in your life?"

[69]

"Yeah, ah'm fallin in love every second week, Da. Ah seem tae piss them off very quickly tho, things goin great, party every night ye know, totally magical, then its like…becomes about normal stuff ye know…canny be bothered wi that, man. Ah'm a bit of a hippy, Dad, alternative, ye know? *Got to keep those good vibrations…*"

He did his arms like waves again.

"Woooohhh."

"Well, as long as your happy son."

Shug felt the wrong impression was being given here. He forgot about the fifty pound for a minute and remembered he was hurt bad by this man. Happy, is it? He nurtured and expanded and connected some bad feelings, brought them to the surface simmering before eruption.

"Happy, is it? Been tae Possil recently? Naw? No exactly happy joyous and free, ye know? Yer dad leave, you did he? Naw, ma granddad's a fuckin soldier compared to you, he's looked out for me while you've been hangin aboot bars in London. Just fuckin took off, whits that about, eh? Did you no miss our kick aboots in the park? Ye said ah was a dead good goalie. Ah was fuckin happy then! Did ye no care about yer wife? Did ye no think ye could take it fuckin handy wi the beer for a few years anyway? "

Shug settled for a minute, unaware of his dad's pain. The jukebox backed up his anger.

Armoured cars and tanks and guns
came to take away our sons,
but every one must stand behind
the men behind the wire!

Shug shouted along.

"Hey! Hawd oan now, hawd oan, Shug. It wasnae fuckin armoured cars that took ye away from me…it was, too much…ah meant to come back, just a bit of space, things calm down, sort myself out. Weeks pass son, ah thought of ye every night, and every night I'd take a few beers, a few hawfs, and ah was powerless, Shug. She, yer maw, wasnae gonny change, just keep on ma case, accuse me, accuse me. I was scared, ah didnae know whit to do, just get rage, fuckin rage, taken over, never meant it ever, but couldn't think once it started, was always going to change, and always it took over me again…ah admit it, ah was scared to came back, time passed and ah thought ye'd both be better without me…broke ma heart."

He threw back the rest of his whiskey.

"Oh aye, Dad, all sorts of reasons there right enough, sorry for doubtin ye, ma mistake." The cynicism wasn't lost on his dad, who shrugged his shoulders, like nothing he could say would be enough now.

Shug got up and walked briskly but drunkenly to the door.

"Shug, for Christs sake sit down a while, or we can meet again, we'll not sort everything today."

"I'll be back, Billy!" Shug called back from the door.

Out in the daylight of Bethnal Green, he looked around for an Ali's Convenience Store, and saw one across the road. Staggering across, he bumped into the side of a bus, but luckily he was bounced like a bar billiard onto the pavement. A notion had taken him over, and he was unable to compromise with his feelings, and not prepared to defer any actions.

In the shop he got himself a quarter bottle of Bell's, twenty Benson, and a plastic football, then misjudged his way back across the road to the pub.

He swung open the door, the ball at his feet, and dribbled his way between tables. Panic spread through the bar, old men clutching at pints with bony hands. A smiling, flat-cap man of about 70 swerved and avoided Shug, remaining happily pissed and with the poise of a ballroom dancer. Some guys seemed happy that at least something was happening "Away the Georgie Best!" shouted one.

Shug started playing keepy-up.

"Watch this Da. You said you'd give me a fiver if ah could dae fifty, remember? Before ye fucked off an leaved us? Wan, two, three, four, five, six, seven…aw fuck…eight." He barged a table, spilling all the drinks but reached the ball. "Nine, sorry aboot that, ten…"

The ball went some distance from him and he ran to reach it. He belted it as forcefully as he could when he got there; it flew hard and fast and full into the face of the barman, an angry small cockney called Davey the Pot, on account of him always having a handle on things.

Stunned with rage and shock, he leapt across the bar,

"You scotch wanker…!" He made for Shug, but just before he was about to grab him Johnny Elvis battered into him with his head, knocking him back to the bar. Old smiley cap was singing happily away nearby, "And I love you so…"

Davey got up again. Shug swung for him but missed and did a full pirouette before slamming into the newly purchased, painted glass window depicting a sleek dolphin flying through the air above the frothy blue sea. Glass cracked and shattered its way out of the space-time continuum, held everyone's attention as it dropped, light blue and green, reflecting the street lights, a mirage of rainbow and whiteness, pointed flat sheets and rough jewels, a terrible beauty…

★★★

Tam looked around the empty ward. He was less numbed by the medication, now that they had gradually trusted him to be safe but unwell rather than dangerous and criminal. His contributions to the group sessions were causing too much laughter and unordered behaviour, so he was barred. Barred from a therapy group. He had a lot of pride in that. For all the well -meaning care and very clever treatments and observations, Tam was aware of a lack of respect for human possibility, and the lack of healing love. Not the nurses' fault, nor the doctors', it was just the mass fear of difference, the chronic phobias around embarrassment that had crippled the public's psyche. Society needed its illusions, or the comfort of being, which would give way to the possibility of becoming, and people weren't ready for that. Tam remembered his pal's words those years before in Glasgow, "Don't let go now, wee man, ye wouldn't want to let go…"

He did try and let go though, to be free to experience, free to feel his full awareness, melt with the physical, mental and spiritual vibrations that he could sense. The obsessions, the birds, the veneers, gave him some order through it all, but the background noise was the totality of life beyond the illusion, and he was a brave man to think he could handle it.

And his pal was here again.

"How's the bold Tam! Long time, mate, ah told ye go easy on the Askit powders, didn't ah?"

"Aye, true enough, looks like you could do wi a few tho?"

"Ah yeah, just wee incident involvin a dolphin, ma dad, and Davey the Pot"

"A dolphin…yer dad?"

"Tell ye more later, thing is, me an you need to get some peace eh? You still got your flat?"

"Aye, it's still there, some social worker sorted out ma rent."

[73]

"Well ma place is too much for me tae think about jist now, any chance ah stay at yours a wee while?"

Tam paused. He was about to put on his orange robe, but thought better and lay it back down.

"Ah'm no ready for this robe yet, you got a jumper or something?"

"Sure, aye, here, ah brought some clothes like ye said, but eh... the flat Tam?"

"Will you promise me wan thing? Ye know it wasnae too much fun last time ye stayed. Never mind fuckin tryin tae work it all oot...ah don't want tae hear about being an no-being, ah don't want tae hear aboot vibes and synchronicity, ah don't want tae hear aboot purpose an fuckin awareness."

"That's a few things, Tam"

"Naw, that's no the thing, the thing is, don't pick up the first drink? Can ye dae that today?"

"Ah will, Tam, ah was thinkin that way anyway."

"Naw, fuck off wi yer thinkin, just gonny no dae that?"

EPISODE FIVE

A message from the dolphins

How Shug finds love when he isn't looking. Ade Adeyobo is met again and uses his skills to understand some eco-dolphins, and how the mystery of life on earth cracks open a little to reveal an evolutionary step towards continuous God-consciousness.

Allihies, Near Castletownbere, West Cork, Ireland

"Heather!" Shug shouted across the field trying to get her attention as she trotted on her white pony slowly down the beach track and across the stream that slowly meandered to the sea. Clear May light framed the sparkling shimmers on the surface of the heaving sea. Shug felt so alive in the beauty of the new grass and wild flowers, orange montbretia, innocent white mayflowers, and the coconut-smelling warm yellow furze that bordered their acre.

"The land that was stolen from my forefathers, the Dochertys' mother earth" – as Shug liked to describe it.

"Heather…!"

She turned and waved, the lightest brightest heavenly wave of a happy child. She couldn't hear him, but it could wait till later, a letter from her granddad saying he was coming over in a couple of weeks' time. She would be pleased; she thought her granddad was so exciting, behaving like he was on holiday for the first time ever. He would swim with her in the sea, try to ride the horse, go exploring, and never say no when it came to requests for indulgence in sugary snacks.

***

It was five years now since Sharon and Shug met at the Highbury Barn meeting of Alcoholics Anonymous. Shug had been sitting at the top table, telling the meeting about his life. He was barely a year sober, and was still speaking with a degree of bravado about some of his drunken escapades.

"I'll tell ye what a black-out is," he had said "A black-out is when you find yourself down in the underground tunnels at three in the morning and you can't remember how you got there and what happened before, battered and bloodied…and still my Higher Power lookin after me."

Sharon was delighted to see him up there recounting his story. He looked much better than that night they first met. She could see the light in his eyes instead of a heavy and soulless watery detachment. She could see he was beginning to understand his disease, and seek to deal with it, look for solutions, how to live well and sober, how to feel the presence of spirit. That was what she first noticed when she saw him on the tube train, his detachment from that spiritual holistic wellbeing; he wasn't at peace, that was for sure, but she could see he was a seeker, not a jobseeker, sure, but a soul that cried out for connection, and all it got was Buckfast, Tenants, whiskey or cheap wine – a seeming shortcut to serenity that took away the ability to connect, that took away God and left the craving ego.

Shug went on, "Ah had ma first drink at the age of 12, a shandy from my Uncle Leo, he would sit there pissed and laughing at family parties, not talking, occasionally breaking into a short burst of song before laughing again. After that drink, it was the first time I remember making my ma and da laugh, as I started singing, pretending to be uncle Leo.

"It felt great to be a part of things, to be an okay wee guy, to make people laugh, and to be free to join in…that's all I wanted really, to be free to join in. Drink made that possible at first…but in the end I was detached from everything and everybody."

Tears had welled a little in Shug's eyes that night, and Sharon could barely contain herself, she felt such warmth for him, and knew things were meant to be. But she also knew you cant go faster than real life, you need to do what's right in the now, you couldn't get ahead of the universe.

"Shug, good to hear you," she had said after the meeting. "I could really identify."

"Thanks, eh, was a bit nervous, and did ah make any sense? Sometimes ah just go on and…do ah know you? Ma memory is pretty bad still, have we met? Feels like we've met…at the Hackney Tuesday night meeting mibbe?"

As Sharon smiled Shug felt that smile was not just happening now, it was a forever smile, met for the first time and would never be able to leave him now it was known. Like the birth of a new addiction he felt the tingling, warm rush from his glad heart to his blissful mind.

He wondered how he could be so affected, just a smile, and the infinity of pure imagination and meaning from her eyes, making him feel like…like God? Like somebody good at least, maybe not God, maybe just the right part of God's jigsaw, fitting as it should with his physical opposite, man and women as the One they strove to be, to become angel beings…love and light …Aye,maybe he fancied her right enough.

"Yeah we've met…my name is Sharon…ring any bells?"

"Sharon? Sharon…for fucks sake…Sharon…ah have your letter here in ma wallet…Sharon, look…" Shug held up the crumpled note. "So we met on the underground the very night ah was talking about just now…? And you wrote to me…and ah wrote back…Did you not get ma letter? Ah wrote fuckin loads…was a

[77]

bit scribbly drunk, right enough. Never mind, here give us a hug, this is pure magic…"

They had an awkward embrace, a mix between AA fellowship and the hope of perhaps more.

"You wrote back to Dzogchen Beara then?" asked Sharon.

"Ah did aye, Dog-chain Beararse, that's right…"

"Aw, its my fault so, I was only there visiting, I should have put my own address on the letter."

"Ah, never mind, probably for the best, not sure what ah was writin aboot anyway, ah'm sure I went over the top…So we were talkin on the tube then? Ye know ah met ma dad that very night the first time in fifteen years? Whits the chances, eh?"

Sharon smiled again. "You couldn't plan it, could you? I love AA for that, I dunno, kind of makes the world small enough for it to make sense, like Watership Down, where all the rabbits…no, maybe more like Postman Pat, Postman Pat and the Earth Adventures of the spirit…"

"Yeah, exactly," Shug had replied, in awe of her quirky musings. "Or Winnie the Pooh even."

One year later Shug jokingly announced to the meeting that he had cleared the *two years before you start a new relationship* suggestion, and that he was now free and would talk to prospective candidates after the meeting. Sharon was first there, of course, and there was easiness to the next steps. From hearing her speak at meetings, his initial infatuation had developed and changed, to an understanding of her whole person. They had met for coffee a lot too, been supportive to each other, free to be honest and open. Different from the drunken lust, weak neediness and selfishness of his drinking days.

Another year passed before Sharon became pregnant. They were living together in her council flat in Holloway and Shug was working as a caretaker, nice and steady, not quite the model worker like Tam, but efficient and reliable enough to get by. When Heather was born Shug's mum and dad met for the first time in seventeen years; they were sociable enough, both so glad for Shug. Tam often visited them too, his drop-in centre was nearby on Seven Sisters Road, where he did a lot of art work. His wood veneer collages were gaining a reputation in the London art world for their craft and for their sublime abstractions from the physical world.

Yes, things seemed to be playing out in a wondrous way. In the days before the dolphins came.

Was it that Heather should have been born a dolphin instead of a human? Was a mix-up possible? It was impossible for them to be sure; all they knew was that a few years after they had moved to Allihies on the West Cork coast of Ireland, things began to become a little strange.

Sharon had been there a number of times before meeting Shug. Her grandfather, Taig O'Sullivan, lived in a run-down farm a few miles inland; she would visit some summers after her mother died, and enjoyed listening to his tales, ghost stories about the wandering copper miners, still working away under the mountain, unable to find away out, and howling *In the name of God the day's work is over, the days work is over!* Tales also of the Children of Lir, how they landed as seals a mile outside Allihies and had settled in the area ever since. Sharon herself, her grandfather said, was a descendant.

One night, well before they moved to West Cork, Shug had a dream of a beach pouring out of a copper kettle and spreading over the land, chimneys belching out smoke high in the hills while white horses bucked and galloped as they were born from very expensive Cadbury cream eggs that rolled towards the beach, the name Sullivan printed in bold on the wrapper. The horses rode into the sea and swam off, becoming dolphins with hands, giving rude vee signs as they moved away from the coast into the deep Atlantic.

Sharon was astounded. "That's Allihies!" she exclaimed. "That must be Allihies. What happened next?"

"Well, it kind of changed then, there was a game of football on the beach, I scored a hat-trick, and the last one was a bicycle kick volley."

"Yep, I think I felt that one." Sharon rubbed her head.

It would just have been a strange dream, far from having Celestine Prophecy meaning to it, until Sharon got a letter from her grandfather. He had been moved to a nursing home, and while there he had sold a number of sites. "I am very loaded Sharon, a proper Celtic Tiger, but it's too late for me now and have little need for it. I can't drink, the bastards. I'd like you to have the old house, and a bit of money to renovate, if you like. You and your girl, and that Scotchman can come and live here, true there's not much to do work wise, but maybe you'll think of something ... but bring me some whiskey and your listening presence."

They jumped at the chance. Shug had always had notions about living in Ireland, and although he was pretty happy being sober, he still sometimes craved some adventure. Sharon had few doubts; her time there was always beautiful, the only thing that gave some respite from her grieving for her parents, and it was sure to make her feel closer to them.

"Beyond our wildest dreams eh?" Shug squeezed Sharon's hand and they accepted God's plan.

***

Heather kicked the horse a little as it slowed in the deep sand,

"Hup! Hup now! Hup Jimmy J!" she shouted, and steered him into the frothy sea. As the water came up over its back she dived and moved under the water like it was her true environment; coming up for air, her big blue eyes looked around as if searching for her missing friends. She dived again and went further out; she was a powerful swimmer for a young girl.

***

Tam spent most of his time at the Dzogchen temple when he was visiting. He initially had caused much annoyance to the serious Buddhist practitioners. As they sat in meditation gazing out the surrounding window over the cliffs to the expanse of the horizon and beyond, Tam often took to cleaning the window with a squeegee and asking for a few bob.

He would also hide in the trees around the Stupa, and occasionally jump out just as he thought the novices had moved into a state approaching clarity of mind.

"Come ahead, ya dobber!" he would scream, then run off into the woods.

But he liked it there really, and in time, when the Rinpoche came to understand him, he began to revere him, recognizing him as the 37th incarnation of Nyoshul Kenpo the Clown, the Buddha's comedian, and destroyer of illusions.

***

Ade Adeyobo opened his mail as he sat on his veranda overlooking the village. A ten-year-old single malt from the Isle of Jura sat on the table.

"Now then, the work goes on, Ade, the good work goes on,"

he said as he poured himself a *wee wan*. Lectures and scientific papers kept him busy (the last one – "Mimicry and Consciousness: the Evolution of the Burundian Macaw" – had caused quite a stir) and he was becoming quite a celebrity, especially since his short time in prison had made international news.

Another conference invitation had come this morning, from the University College Cork, Ireland. "Understanding Animal Behaviours – A Seminar for Applied Animal Psychology Professionals". A paid trip too, accommodation and travel. Things must be looking up for the Irish.

Ade mused over the invite. The little he knew about Ireland had been from his time in Glasgow, a riot at a sheep-dog trial because one dog was called Bobby Sands and another Red Hand. But that's not Ireland, he reminded himself, that's the a tragic-comedy of the West of Scotland.

He decided. "Yes well, I'd like to go, a few Guinness and so forth, and that wonderful music, perhaps a good place for green politics too…"

★★★

Heather felt herself lifted from below, and was thrown out of the water, turning in the air and splashing back in; a common dolphin swam close beside her and she felt herself put her arm round its fin and be carried along. All the time it looked at her and chattered and whistled, in a way that Heather could not understand. She listened and tried to remember though, and then was carried back by a dolphin and let go of in the shallow water. Quickly she called Jimmy J over and climbed on. She galloped back to the cottage, dismounted and ran up to her room where she took out an empty jotter and began writing.

[82]

"Whistle whistle click clic click clic clic whistle clic clik whistle…." Page after page she wrote, nearly every day going out again to the sea and returning with more messages. It became known to the local newspaper, then the television came to see. RTE's *Nationwide* did a piece on her, "Heather and the Dolphins: the incredible child of the sea".

Shug and Sharon were so worried but could not stop her from escaping out whenever she could to swim with the Dolphins.

As she wrote, Shug and Sharon argued downstairs.

"All your stupid talk, Shug, its got to her, she doesn't know what's real and what's not…all the mysterious *woo woo stories,* it's got to stop, maybe it's fine for you but not a child, you have her talking to Dolphins for Gods sake…"

"Ma stupid talk is it? How come me? Didn't ye no say Allihies was some kind of magical place by the sea? Children of Lir? What the fuck's that?"

Sharon stormed off crying. Shug felt powerless and couldn't think what was the right thing to do, so he threw a mug at the wall, then sat head in hands and prayed for help.

★★★

Ade's flight touched down in Cork, to the applause of the passengers. This puzzled him a little, well done for landing safely? A great achievement? How lucky had he been?

He had three days to spend in Ireland, but would be busy with the conference for most of that time. He hoped to see some of the scenery though, perhaps, he joked to himself, see St Patrick roaming in the gloaming with a shamrock in his hand.

He went off to his Hotel and began preparing for his contribution, "Inter-species Communication in the Age of Global Warming – What are our Earth Companions Saying?"

He had built up some evidence that animals communicate their distress at changes to their climate and environment. Indian elephants had recently been seen kicking cars and charging at petrol stations. Penguins in the south Atlantic were shouting there heads off at passing tankers. The monkeys of the Canary Islands were pick-pocketing the tourists and displaying all their currency on the branches of trees. And of course the macaws who were rampaging and harassing people. The Government of Burundi was seriously considering bringing in anti-social behaviour orders for birds in some parts of the country.

There had been no evidence, however, of constructive criticism from the animals, no clear message regarding solutions, or how we might cooperate.

Ade put away his source materials and tried to relax. Opening the mini-bar he discovered a nice selection of whiskeys, and he began comparing them as he sat in front of the TV.

Podge and Rodge, then Father Ted – the taxi driver had advised him to look out for those programmes to get a good feel for Irish culture. He laughed his way though, much taken by the antics of the priests. Back in some parts of Burundi they were just starting out on the Catholic journey, so it was interesting to see it here in its last days of decay.

Ade began to nod off, well topped up with the miniatures, and was tired from the journey. He was startled awake though from a familiar voice on the TV.

"Aye, she goes fur a swim most days, an the dolphins always come and speak to her…naw, have no idea whit they're sayin, ah don't speak clicky whistle language ye know? But she writes it all down…"

Ade rubbed his eyes in amazement, was it himself? Yes! That's him alright. Ade looked at the scruffy blond-haired Scot on the TV, standing before a cottage with the sea in the background.

"Ha ha, my friend, the bold Shug...and a problem with the animals again...in...Allihies, West Cork, I see. I must go surprise my distant soul brother, perhaps his clan elder has summoned me ...ha ha"

Ade set off the following morning. His presentation wasn't till the following day and he could hold himself back no longer from taking part in this happening. He hired a car and set off around 10am, Cork to Bandon to Bantry, through Glengarriff past Castletownbere and on to Allihies. The difference of the scenery, and anticipation of the changes, kept him mesmerized and alert. As he drove down towards the coast of Glengarriff he felt again his love for this planet. A pointed mountain rose high above a peninsula that reached out its rocky form into its friend the sea. An old forest of oak and birch and elm spread like an ancient glory across the mountainsides. A few times he nearly drove off the road, frightened by the speed of the overtaking cars as they sped by in an angry hurry. But he kept his cool; his pace was steady, like a magnet was pulling him onwards, unstoppable and precise.

The last time they had written to each other was a few years ago, when Shug's child was born, Heather..."So this was Heather speaking with the dolphins," he thought.

★★★

Outside in the midday rain, Shug was busy shifting some rocks to repair a stone wall that bordered their land. The ground was very sodden after the winter; it hadn't stopped raining hardly since the beginning of October, and only now in May was it beginning to dry as the days began to warm. It could be hot even, hot like the

[85]

days in Burundi almost. The days of wearing a dufflecoat on the beach in the middle of summer seemed to be over.

Shug loved the simplicity of his life now, whatever was happening; he was making small changes in tune with spirit, in tune with his inner-self, in tune with the land. Before the dolphins came, he was for the first time free of searching, doubt and confusion. The importance of the small incidents of life had been lost on him before, but now he could chat about the weather, take an interest in the ingredients of his food, slow down. He could open boxes of cereal properly, not tearing into them in an unconfident, impatient fit of desperation, but checking where to tear, tearing one step at a time.

"If only the dolphins would stop," he thought. Tam was trying to help in his own way: he had the whole temple meditating on blessings of peace and love to the dolphins; sometimes they could be seen while they looked out to sea, and their chants carried all their good intention towards them.

★★★

Ade felt a certain surrealness as he continued round the coast towards Allihies. He was not used to being so close to the sea and the cliffs, and after three hours driving he began to feel a little shaky, like it wasn't him driving, like it wasn't him thinking, like his hands were separate, like some unspecified fear crept into his mind. He experienced this a few times these days, and he knew what it was, withdrawal. He started to sweat and his heart raced. There was nowhere in sight to get drink, surely round the corner a pub, surely the next corner, surely the next corner, God, how far to go now...

As he drove through a gap in the hills a magnificent panorama presented itself beneath him, a scattering of cottages, white and pink and blue, and then he could make out a village clustered on top of a hill. The sea frothed in a magnificent whiteness around the jaggy coast, and stretched out below was the curve of a golden sandy beach.

"To the village," Ade thought, "I must go to the village."

★★★

Shug lay down another rock, and listened to his body: *time to rest,* he heard clearly. And a little less clearly, *time for a plate of sausages, bacon, and eggs.* Sharon had gone out with Heather, no doubt trying to make her feel better after yesterday's arguments. Shug decided to take a stroll up to the village and treat himself to dinner in the local pub. He enjoyed his own company these days, but it was good to get out occasionally. The locals enjoyed his company too; his accent helped, as the Billy Connolly effect was in full swing out here, and even the mildest of comedic utterances was greeted with delighted laughter.

★★★

Ade pulled up outside the pub in the centre of the village. It was misty and getting dark outside, a constant drizzle falling. Ade felt better already, seeing the cosiness through the window, the cosiness and the shining bottles neatly arranged behind the bar.

He pushed the door open, still a little shakily. He had no time to worry about peoples reactions to a stranger, but instead went straight to the bar. "Hi, I would like a glass of Guinness please and a whiskey." His hands shook as he counted the change. The other clients noticed this and he was one of them already, accepted; the fellowship of the suffering alcoholic was weak, but it was there.

Ade took a seat near the window and gulped down his drinks; again, the others glanced at each other, impressed.

He bought another and sat back down, a smile coming alive on his face. The whole pub began to smile; to see a hangover defeated was a wonderful thing

A man of about 60 sitting at the counter, the look of a sheep farmer on him, turned to Ade.

"Grand day, eh? Bout time too…"

"Yes, it was dry for a while earlier, just after two I think… beautiful scenery around here ."

"Yes, yes, ner be looking at it much but tis I believe…you'll be on holiday? Or looking for work, need a bit of help in the fields myself…"

"Well, neither really, I was visiting the university in Cork. I am an academic."

"Oh, Cork, so your from Cork, norside is it? Was there last year, saw a blackman like yourself, he was selling the Evening Echo."

"Ha! No, I am from Africa, a country called Burundi." Ade took a sip of whiskey and smiled.

"Africa, eh? Well fair play to ye boy!" The farmer raised his glass and continued. "The man from Africa, in the parish of Allihies, Beara Abu! "

It was quiet again for a minute before Ade spoke again.

"I saw this village on the television last night. Do you know about the dolphin story?"

"The dolphin story…" the man thought, "Ah…its the Kerry hoars ye want, Fungi is it? Well you're on the wrong piece of land, my African friend, its Dingle yer after for the dolphin."

Another man sitting close by joined in.

[88]

"No, Michael, he's right, was on last night, the sober Scot, lives down by the beach road, his daughter's been talking to the dolphins or something, was on Nationwide last night right enough."

"That's it yes. That Scotsman, he is my friend! You know where I can find him? " Ade asked excitedly.

The second man nodded to the door behind Ade as it swung open. Shug looked up from his Buy and Sell, Ade looked at him, and nodded like a local.

"Fuck! Is it ..? Mr Ade Adeyobo?"

Ade stood up, arms opened...

Shug! The master of the Glaswegian macaws, ha ha!"

They hugged and felt their energies mingle again, but unlike that first time in Africa, the healing worked both ways, like they were both meeting in the middle of a bridge, a bridge to mutual support, cooperation...*do not compete, compose*...was the thought they both had.

The two friends walked back to the cottage through the dark after they had eaten. Ade didn't even suggest getting a carry-out to take home.

Sharon and Heather were just back too. Sharon had built a roaring fire and they were both sat in front of it, Heather busy drawing while Sharon glanced through a magazine.

"Sharon, this is my friend Ade, I told you all about Ade, didn't I? "Shug beamed.

"Of course, the Macaws, of course, I've heard lots about you, welcome Ade, welcome." Sharon got up from the fire. "And this is Heather...say hello, Heather."

"Hello Mr Ade...have you come to speak to the dolphins?"

"Oh Heather, sssh about the Dolphins just now, pet," her mum said.

"Hi Heather, it's okay, Sharon, actually I would be interested, maybe you can show me your jotter later? I saw you on TV last night, your a very famous girl."

"Yes, the man with the big tie was so stupid…"

"Okay, Heather, that's enough, he was just doing his job…although I agree he was a bit silly."

Sharon brought tea and Shug's home-made scones while they chatted by the fire.

Ade explained how he got here, with Shug nodding all the way, fully understanding the long-distance connection the men still had, unsurprised by the wonder of intention.

"So, we have both changed a lot since those days my friend, and what about Tam, he recovered from his whitey okay?"

"Yeah, ha ha, he did, had a few more on the way tho, but he's settled down a bit, he's not far, just a few miles round the hill at the Buddhist Temple, we can call in and see him tomorrow if ye like."

"Well, if it's possible we can pick him up. Would you like to come to my presentation in Cork? All of you please, I need to go home again next day and it would be great to see more of you."

Shug and Sharon looked at each other, and said with one voice, "Yes."

"A trip to Cork to hear a magnificent green activist, what could be better?" Sharon added, smiling warmly to Shug, while noticing her broken Serenity Prayer mug lying on the table. She scowled, but then it was over, a passing scowl, the best sort.

Ade retired to bed not too late, to rest before his early morning trip back to Cork, but he took some time to look at Heather's jotter as he lay on the camp bed, while outside the rain lashed at the window and strong gusts of wind howled around the yard. "Mm…," he thought again. "Do not compete, compose."

In the morning Ade seemed very happy and enthusiastic. He asked if Shug would drive as he wanted to work a little on his presentation. He scribbled furiously, reading and rereading Heather's jotter the whole way there, only stopping to chat briefly with Tam, and to wave back at the Rinpoche, who stood outside the temple and shouted "The blessings of the Buddha " as they drove off. Ade also made a couple of calls, and again seemed delighted at the result.

At the university Ade arranged for his friends to have front row seats, and then rushed off to confirm what time he would be speaking as well as to arrange something that he knew would come as a surprise to everyone.

Around three in the afternoon Ade was introduced by the university head: "Mr Adeyobo is a man of great courage...his time in prison... on trumped up charges that he attacked some loggers with a team of angry Scottish macaws was ridiculous, but they cannot besmirch his scientific endeavours...his attention to detail and his commitment to telling the truth about global climatic changes and how they affect not just man, but the whole animal kingdom...ladies and gentlemen, Mr Ade Adeyobo..."

Shug, Tam, Sharon and Heather applauded and cheered as Ade went to the podium.

"Thank you, thank you, I am just a humble worker, thank you."

At this Tam cheered even louder and shouted, "Up the humble workers!"

Ade smiled to Tam and continued.

"Thank you, Mr Fahy, for that introduction, although I must point out, without fear of litigation, the macaws were real, and perhaps not entirely Scottish but definitely speakers of the Glaswegian tongue. In fact, as we swooped on the loggers the cry was *Get intae them, get intae them!* And indeed we did!"

"C'mon the macaws," Shug shouted.

Mr Fahy looked over, in slight mental discomfort.

Ade continued, "I had the pleasure yesterday of visiting a most beautiful part of your country, the Beara Peninsula in West Cork, and what I saw there has made me make some changes to my presentation, indeed, I have changed it completely. I intended to speak in a general way about recent studies relating to changes in animal behaviour, with a relevance to world climatic changes.

"But I would like to share with you some feelings, feelings that grew in me last night and today as I tried to decode the messages from the Allihies dolphins, brought to us and recorded by my little friend Heather…take a bow, Heather."

Heather stood and bowed as the delegates applauded politely, but with some annoyance.

"Last night I began to read the clicks and whistles that Heather recorded. I have looked at dolphin language patterns before, of course, and we are now quite sure that there is a complexity of communications beyond any other species. But what happened to me last night was not scientific, it was not decoding, it was not rational, but it is the truest thing I have ever heard, and I mean heard."

The crowd looked surprised, but also mesmerized as Ade spoke.

"I would like to introduce you to, someone you may be already familiar with, Mr Noel Clancy of the Jigtown Reels."

The audience looked on in astonishment as a bearded Noel Clancy came on to the stage with his flute.

"Thank you, Mr Clancy, for agreeing at such short notice to be with us today."

The crowd shuffled and whispered to each other.

"Four Green Fields," somebody shouted from the back, to much laughter.

Ade spoke quietly to Mr Clancy, and showed him a few pages

of the jotter, pointing out certain parts as the musician nodded with understanding.

"Ladies and gentlemen, can we have some quiet while Mr Clancy plays a new composition."

Slowly at first the flautist moved through a number of melodies and rhythms and then picked up pace to begin a symphony of classical sounds, swept together, rising and falling, from melodic beauty to shattering broken points of noise. The audience gasped as he turned the pages of the jotter and seemed to know what came next without hardly reading it. There were sections of gentle murmuring sweetness and melody that evoked terrible loss and sadness, and parts with great uplifting hope. After around ten minutes it came to an end, seemingly unfinished. The flautist sat trembling and looked over to Ade, who approached and hugged him. "That was beautiful, thank you," he said quietly, before turning to the shocked and awed audience.

"The voice of the dolphins..." Ade began to cry, his sobs the only sound in the whole auditorium.

There...is a title to this music too...I will check and recheck with all the previous studies, of course, but it seems clear to me... it is called, and of course, it can only be approximate, *Grow Seaweed in the Sky*. Seaweed in the sky – my feeling is trees, my feeling is that means we must grow trees"

Shug was first to stand up, then Sharon, Heather, Tam, the people behind them, slowly the whole audience stood and applauded, some crying, others cheering, while Ade nodded solemnly then smiled.

The humility of homo sapiens was evident that day, and the comfort of knowing came upon all there: knowing that we are not alone in the mystery, we are not alone in the mystery.

EPILOGUE

In which Shug and Tam are interviewed by Mr Gay Byrne on the RTE Late Late Show.

"Well now…it's not very often I can say on this show that my next guests saved the world from total catastrophe, and I'm not talking about Superman or comic book characters here, but of two gentlemen from Glasgow, whose interest in bird watching and a chance meeting with renowned eco-warrior Ade Adeyobo, led to an understanding that the future of the planet necessitated wholesale global reforestation.

"Since the words of the dolphins of Allihies, County Cork, were translated, three billion – yes, billion! – trees have been planted worldwide. A ten-foot rise in sea level now looks to have been averted, and temperatures are set to stabilize by 2025.

"A movie of the events starring Sean Connery and Billy Connolly is due out next month, and the lads have been on a whirlwind speaking tour, meeting presidents and addressing thousands of rapturous people from China to California.

"Ladies and gentlemen, Shug Docherty and Tam McLaverty!"

(Audience breaks into applause as Shug and Tam, both wearing Glasgow Celtic Twitchers' Society t-shirts walk on stage.)

"Welcome, welcome, welcome, my friends…Have a seat, lads…listen to that appreciation…

"From a humble background in a Glasgow housing estate to saving Planet Earth! How does it feel, boys?"

Shug: "Aye, it's okay really, no bad."

Tam: "No very good to be honest, Mr Gay. Ah'v been getting a lot of hate mail and wish the whole thing never happened…letters from wee ladies in Aberdeen, saying stuff like 'It was getting a wee bit warmer here and ye Wegian scum go and spoil it all!' or "Tim bastards, who wants a fuckin green world, fuck off' from the Govan Orange Order. It's affected ma mental health to be honest."

(Shug pats Tam on the shoulder..)

Gay: "Well, some people don't realize just how lucky we are … the fools. Shug, did you ever doubt your daughter Heather when she said the dolphins were talking to her? A little fatherly worry perhaps?"

Shug: "Well, furstly can ah say its good to be on the Late Night! Ma da used tae watch it."

Gay: "Is he here tonight?"

Shug: "Yeah, da, ma mum, Sharon and Heather all here tonight!"

(The four wave from front seats in the audience.)

Gay: "Tam, you have well wishers here, I see!"

(Camera focus on about ten Buddhist monks; all seem inebriated, clashing symbols and blowing horns and shouting *Peaceful Mind* before bursting into uproarious laughter.)

Gay: "Now, now, lads, lets settle down. I can see you're happy people, and good to see you all, a little less symbols and horns, please. Where were we, yes the dolphins?"

Shug: "It was of course, Gay, a stressful time, but ye know what, ah handed it over, hand everything over, whit does it mean? Hows it gonny work oot in the end? Hand it fuckin over."

Gay: "You still see the dolphins?"

Shug: "Naw, ah'm afraid not, think they probably gone to the Caribbean, spreading the word, we miss them tho, especially Heather."

Gay: "A surprise, a surprise, we all love a surprise…behind us we have a big screen and somebody wants to say hello to you!"

Screen appears. "Whistle whistle clickkkk clickkkkk …."

Gay: "I believe you know Ade, here with one of Heather's dolphin friends!"

Ade: "Hallo, Tam…hallo Shug, good to see you are on TV now and so famous! I am working now with a few of the Allihies dolphins…"

Tam, Shug: "Ade, big man, good tae see ye! The real world saver!"

Ade: "Not without my Glasgow Twitcher friends! One of the dolphins wants to say something to you."

Dolphin: "Click whistle cliiiiiick whistle…..click click click."

Shug: "Excellent, whats he saying?"

Ade: "He`s singing… *Thank you for the trees, those lovely trees, those special trees you gave me.*"

Audience: "Awwwww!"

Gay: "Awww, magnificent creature."

Dolphin: "Clicky clicky whistle whistle long click."

Gay: "What's he saying now, Ade?"

Ade: "Ehm, something about… *Any fishfingers mate? Ah'm gaspin fur a gud fuckin fishfinger*…ah I see…they are joking with the Scottish accent, haha, clever!"

(Audience laughs).

Tam: "Ye still in touch wi the nacaw, Ade?"

Ade: "Yes Tam! He appeared on an African Network reality TV program recently called Animals Gone Mental – though I'm afraid he's never got over his drug addiction issues. He longs to be back in Paisley and have a plentiful supply of hash and temazepam, he speaks of little else…"

Gay: "Sorry, Ade, I must just cut in there. I'm sure you'll understand we can't be talking about birds and drug addiction, important subject though it is…The goodly people Ireland are not quite ready for that…"

[97]

(Audience somber applause.)

Gay: "So, Tam, what's become of you, I see your friends in robes."

(Camera cuts to monks standing up and chanting "Wee Tam! Rinpoche! Wee Tam! Rinpoche!"

(Audience, including a few nuns and priests and older farmer couples, clap along in time.)

Gay: "Okay, okay boys...You're popular Tam! Are you still living down in Beara at the monastery?"

Tam: "No, Mister Gay, I was eh kicked out of there, but ah'm not far away. Ahve a caravan along the cliff a bit, on Alex the Donkey Whisperer's land★. I help him out with like, some whisperin an stuff."

Gay: "Fantastic, so still in the same line of business..."

(Audience applause, Tam red faced looking to the floor, slight smile breaking through.)

Gay: "And yourself, Mr Shug Docherty, life being good to you? You speak of some of your own struggles during the adventure the, lets see, Gaian miracle, things settle down for you still?"

Shug: "Indeed, Gay, one day at a time, very busy wi the GCTS. We huv 150, 000 members now, the best supported bird-watchin group in the world, Scottish champions the last three years in a row, though sure there's a sectarian divide in Glasgow still. The Rangers' rnithologists were recently found out to be cheating, downloading pictures of birds they didn't see and claiming them for themselves, been demoted to division three now in spottin burds competition against the like of the Brechin Birdies and The Dumbarton Seagull Army...a faw fae Heights awrite...plus ma

★ *Alex The Donkey Whisperer, and Animal Refuge, Beara. For every 100 books sold a bag of donkey food will be donated to the refuge*

[98]

family keep me on the right track of course."

(Shug waves to family.)

Gay: "Come on up on stage…come come…Mr and Mrs Docherty, Sharon, Heather…the Buddha boys, come on up too!"

(All gather round Shug and Tam. The Buddhists start shouting.)

"Lets all do the huddle! Lets all do the huddle! Na na na na!, Na na na na!"

(Everyone puts arm round each other, Gay joins in, whole audience start doing the Huddle.)

"Gaia does the huddle Gaia does the huddle na na na na ……."

(Theme tune. Credits roll. End of Show.)

ACKNOWLEDGEMENTS

This book is in some way an outcome of a writing assignment given at the Creative Writing group above the radical bookshop on Kingsland High Street, Hackney. *Write a story about a Parrot*, or something like that. I'm finished it now, twenty-two years later, here in West Cork via the Clonakilty Writing group. There's a time and a place, in fact there's a few times and a few places, and the finale of the book owes more to wild swimming in Lough Hyne and walks through the woods with my wonderful partner Helen, definitely a shelter from the storm.

Thanks to Scotland…yes I left on the bus pretty soon after being able to…but I always return, and love your ways, your humour and your Tablet.

Thanks to Psoken Word, and De Barra's, Clonakilty; freedom of expression really opened up for me there. Thanks to friends, to Nick, Fransesco, Brendan, Mary Rose,Jeff, Stu, Moe, John O'R, Moze, Claire, Joe, Michael, Afric, Sean, Traze. and more.

Thanks to John the Bank and Painter Brian for guiding me back onto the path of sanity when I wander.

Thanks To all at the writing group and to Clonakilty Library. To Will Helps for being able to draw a disdainful looking antelope, and so skilfully visualising and drawing the Glasgow Celtic Twitchers' Society. To Maurice Sweeney for telling me it was worth it. To Neil K Henderson, author of Absurd Scottish Titles such as *An English Summer in Scotland: Other Unlikely Events* and *Fish Worshipping for Beginners* (both available on Amazon).

To Aidan , always love.

To Uncle Leo for taking me to Scottish Cup Final 1975 and introducing me to Glasgow Celtic, who somewhere down through the Hampden dust and in front of the thousands of tall people, were playing football. For West Ham Dave…you were right about that sobriety Keystone! Thanks. For Eamonn F, On the Rest and be Thankful, your fantastic laughter ended, hope the book is available in the parallel universe you're in now !

For my Dad. If I knew then what I know now my appreciation of your working life, wit, and character would be ringing in your ears. For my Mum, because I can remember how you looked when I made you laugh or smile, and how that made me feel still resides within.

And for anyone thinking of puttin oot a wee story…That book's no gonny write itssell ye know. Get crackin if that's what yer intae.

The world needs more random sillyness and less organised dogmas, and more trees, of course, and a gameshow involving Glaswegian macaws singing sectarian chants while…(STOP! ENOUGH! – Ed).

Lightning Source UK Ltd.
Milton Keynes UK
UKHW01f0608120618

324105UK00001B/53/P